CD Grimes
Book eleven 2 parts
A Local Murder
(originally: A Local Affair)
Don't Push

CD throws a New Year party. A flashy woman attends, then is found dead in the morning at the community center.

Pt. Two, Sean and Lorna find a body in Estero Bay.

<u>Critic comment</u>
<u>2014</u> I find the first story, *A Local Murder*, to be rather a good read.

This is a partially revised edition, and was matched with the original. I find it reads much better. The characters are well-distinguished and consist of types we all know.

A woman crashes a New Year Party, then is found murdered.. It eventuates that she was a famous artist who painted male nudes. The question is; was one of her models the killer?

Moulton has stated that the solution was stated near the beginning of the book, and that was true. I did not spot it.

Actually, quite good. ****

Don't Push was more or less standard fare. While it was readable, it was a bit too ordinary for my personal tastes. ***

Arthur H. Renquist 22-11-2014

CD Grimes
Book eleven
2 parts
A Local Murder
Don't Push

(c) 1991 & 2019 by C. D. Moulton

This is a work of fiction. Any resemblances to persons living or dead is purely coincidental.

Contents

About the Author

CD began writing fiction in 1984 and has more than 300 books published as of 3/15/16 in SciFi, murder, orchid culture and various other fields.

He now resides Gualaca, Chiriqui, Panamá, where he continues research into epiphytic plants and plays music with friends. He loves the culture of the indigenous people and counts a majority of his closer friends among that group. He funds those he can afford through the universities where they have all excelled. "The Indios are very intelligent people, they are simply too poor (in material things and money.) to pursue higher education."

CD loves Panamá and the people, despite horrendous experiences (Free e-book; *Fading Paradise*). He plans to spend the rest of his life in the paradise that is Panamá

CD is involved in research of natural cancer cure at this time. It has proven effective in all cases, so far. It is based on a plant that has been in use for thousands of years, is safe, available, and cheap. He was cured of a serious lymphoma with use of the plant, *Ambrosia peruviana*.

Information about this cure is free on the FaceBook page Ambrosia peruviana for cancer. CD asks only that all who try it please report on its effectiveness on that group.

A Local Murder
Prologue

It was good to be back home again after that big mess up in Nicely. The orchids I brought back were doing fine and the new awards were all in the case. My beautiful wife, Alma, had to go to that orchid show by herself because of the case, but the next International Exhibition was to be held in San Diego, California, in February. I damned well meant to go to that one!

Things were as normal as they ever were. Christmas was over, the kids had managed to break all their toys, we had company the whole time from before Christmas until now. Mom and Dad (mine) and Mama and Poppa (Alma's) had spent the time with us at the Bonita Springs place. Everybody had a nice suntan and everyone was going home on the second – day after tomorrow.

1989 ended with record cold for two days. Temperatures were generally in the 80's except for a few days here and there. It got into the low fifties once since the freeze, but the next afternoon it was into the low 70's and was in the high 70's the following day.

Jim Barrow, my boatman, Paulo and Lou Sanchez, my housekeeper and outside gardener, Len Stewart and his live-in girlfriend, Mike Nelson, the owner of the private airport where I keep my jet in Sarasota and Shirley and Tony Jacobi, head of the Crane crap that I own 51% of had been to the Englewood place all day, and would have their own New Year's Eve party. Alma and I thought we should meet our new neighbors in Bonita Springs, so a community party would be the best opportunity. We were generally quiet on New Years, so it would be unusual.

Cal Jones and his wife, Wilma, would go up to the Englewood place.

Cal works for the Florida Highway Patrol and has been a close friend since I moved here. Dave, my author friend (He writes the "Maita" SF series books), would probably come to Bonita Springs. The weather was going to be beautiful and there would be plenty of room outside of my "A" frame house for as many as show up. There's plenty of space here. No one would be bothered by any noise.

We'd invited everyone in the small subdivisions close to our own place and quite a lot of them said they'd come. We decided to leave our own kids with Paulo and Lou. Alma had kept their kid over Christmas so they could visit their families. Now it was their turn.

Alma, Lou and Wilma have some system where they each take care of everyone else's kids at times so everybody gets a little rest, now and then. There are times I think those kids have no idea of who their real parents are, but they seem happy enough.

I was wondering what my neighbors were like when Dave came in from the bay in my little boat with a mess of crabs and a few sheepshead, which he cleaned at the dock while the crabs boiled. He finished the fish and crabs, cleaned the place, and came over to the greenhouse, where I was wondering whether or not to use his variety of Lc. Peggy Huffman on the Blc. Don DeMichaels. He said he'd already made the cross and it was already in flasks.

"I think your little party's gonna be interesting. The way a couple of those damned idiots were acting out there, I wouldn't be surprised if somebody didn't end up murdered!"

"I think I can do without that kind of prediction. It would be kinda nice to go through a year without any murders. At least, the first few months."

"Yeah. Ain't gonna happen. It'll get worse before it gets better. You probably won't get through the first week without at least one."

I wish he'd learn to keep his mouth shut!

Chapter one

There were about a hundred people at the party. I met them all and would remember their names, a very good habit in the detective business. I would recognize and speak to all of them whenever we met again, anywhere.

Dave grinned when Bill and Betty Kocsis came in and said Bill was one of the two who were about to come to blows out in the bay earlier. I hoped the one he had been arguing with didn't show up – or that they would have better sense than to renew the argument there, if he did. I wouldn't hesitate to tell them both to leave if they pulled any of that crap at my place.

When Jim Tooney came in, Dave said he was the other one in the argument, but the two didn't pay any attention to each other, in a sort of studied way.

I noticed a bit of a stir among the guests when a very well-built, dark, purposefully sexy woman came in. I noticed the women all seemed to snub her and all the men looked, but none except the bachelors actually spoke to her, which seemed to make the women even madder.

I'm used to women who play those games. So is Alma, who has her own way to handle such things. She was standing beside me when the woman came to meet us. The woman looked me over from head to foot and back again and gave me a very obvious look.

Alma laughed out loud, then said, "I'm Alma and this is CD. He's my husband and, dear, you don't have anything like what it takes, so have fun trying!

"I have to mingle, so you entertain our guests, Love."

"Uh, I'm Bonnie. Bonnie Patrick. I just look too much. I

don't touch. Married men. Unless they...?"

"You're a bit obvious with it, I'm afraid," Alma replied. "I really don't mind. I just wish Jim was here. You'd love him and he'd love you back!

"Have fun!"

"Who's Jim?" Bonnie asked. She didn't get mad at Alma, which wasn't really that unusual, because Alma had her beat in every department, and she knew it.

"He's my boatman, Jim Barrow."

"If that woman recommends him, I think I'd like to meet him!" She grinned. "I think she'd be very hard to please. I'm not."

"Oh, that's too bad! I always like a challenge. When Jim's here, sometime, I'll send him over to your place."

She grinned again, gave me a droopy-eyelidded look and swayed off into the guests. I noticed Jim Tooney went right to her – and Bill Kocsis looked as though he could gleefully murder him. Betty Kocsis looked as though she could gleefully murder both Bill and Bonnie if not Tooney.

I shook my head, and Selma Wentworth, an unattached and rather attractive woman in her early thirties, said, "She's quite a bit of work, isn't she?"

"I'm afraid I don't know her, but she seems the type who was raised to be the beauty queen and to have anything she wanted. She was spoiled rotten. She turns it on and off and doesn't really mean it. She likes being the center of atten-tion."

"You wish! She keeps the whole trailer park in a dither. Deliberately."

"Competitive with other women for attention?"

"She has affairs with anyone who'll go along with her. I saw you watching Bill and Betty. She recently had her fling with him. Betty said she'd cut her tits off for her if she ever even looked at him again.

"Steve Keene was just before that and Sean McMullins before that. Rumors with Sean. Could be, but I sort of doubt it. Like with you, she has 'way too much competition. Lorna has her beat as to looks and personality, not to mention, Sean's the rock-solid type.

"I don't speak to her. Several of us women don't. She knows she'd better stay away from our husbands or special friends.

"Jennie Allen's in our not-so-little group now. She's another member of the `I'll kill the bitch' club."

"Who's Jennie Allen? I've met a Paul and Winnie Allen."

"You remember names, don't you? I wish I could.

"Jennie's Paul's mother. She lives with Paul and Winnie. She only spoke to Bonnie once, to tell her if she ever even looked crooked at Paul again she would end up dead meat, so be sure her will was up to date,

"Karl and Edna Forbes and Connie Peters are the rest of our group here tonight, though the Forbes are members of any 'agin it' group – and, to tell the truth, I don't care to be around the type.

"It may seem awfully petty to you for us to get together to agree to not speak to a person, but we're the only ones in the park who haven't had trouble with her.

"There's not much else to do around here if you don't fish or work."

"I'd be afraid of a woman like that. What with AIDS and herpes and all that, it just isn't worth it. I told her I'd introduce her to Jim Barrow, my boatman. He isn't in the least selective."

"Jim Barrow, from Englewood? I know him. He's a

dream of a man. I think he could handle her. Very well."

We talked a bit about Englewood, then she wandered off. I saw Bonnie talking to Dave, who said something that made her turn very red, then she stalked angrily off. I wandered over and asked him what happened.

"She said she'd read about the book I dedicated the royalties from to AIDS hospice financing. She was rubbing all over me and acting like some very badly-drawn character in a pulp thriller, so I asked her if she'd been tested for HIV antibodies. Seemed to upset her."

I laughed and went to meet Bat and Kitty Lorris, who grow a few orchids. I showed them through the greenhouses, along with Dave and Sylvia Weitz. When we got back outside, Mac McMullins was reading Bonnie the riot act.

Mac was Sean's father. He was naturally a bit loud, but this was louder than usual. I went over and told him he could shut up or leave.

"Do you know what that she-bitch did?!"

"I don't *care* what she did! You're a guest here and she's a guest here. Whatever she did, it wasn't here, I don't want to hear it, and neither do my other guests. If you can't conduct yourself in a civilized manner, you can leave. Save this kind of crap for another place and another time. I won't go to your home and make an ass out of myself. Please return the favor!"

He stared hard at me, then burst out laughing. "I really did ask for that, didn't I? I'll try to act like I know some manners, young fella. Gimme another chance?"

I grinned back and he went over to talk with Norm and Pat Shultz, but I noticed several women gathering in a little group. I pointed to them and Alma went over. They talked a minute, then the women separated. Alma came over to me.

"They were plotting to catch her out of the light and beat hell out of her. I told them she was only here looking for attention and they were playing her game, her way, to perfection.

"I told them she was making fools out of them, then I said the one thing that sort of tramp couldn't tolerate was being ignored, so the easiest way to ruin the evening for her would be to totally ignore her or make her play another game. If she couldn't cause a stir, she'd probably go to a bar somewhere where she could be what she's about to become here – the center of attention."

I noticed how the evening was getting decidedly more pleasant almost immediately. The women seemed in some kind of conspiracy with Alma. They pointedly tried to be pleasant to Bonnie, which had her confused. I even heard Jean Billings tell her husband, Tom, to get poor Bonnie another drink. The one she had was empty.

Then she walked away and let Tom stand there with Bonnie. That confused Bonnie *and* the men, who didn't know what was going on, so avoided Bonnie. She was left with no one but Jim Tooney after a little while. I saw her going out toward her car about eleven thirty or so. I was talking to Selma Wentworth at the time, and mentioned it.

"Your wife's a genius! She's a jewel!" Selma said. "She said for all the women to be solicitous and sweet to Bonnie and it would scare her off. It worked!"

"Alma's good at psychology, but I could figure that one. She wants to be the center of attention. You take away all her little props – which are jealous women – and she doesn't know what to do, so she leaves. It confused the men so much they were scared to have anything to do with her, which only added to her frustration."

"Whatever, it worked – and Alma's the one who thought it up. I think your wife and I will probably become very good friends!"

I spent the rest of the evening in mingling and talking with everyone there. The party started breaking up around one, and everyone was gone by a quarter after two – and no one drove who was even a little drunk. I watched all of them carefully and had three couples driven home by neighbors. They could come back after their cars in the morning. I'm a bit of a prude when it comes to driving drunk. Not from MY party, you won't!

We decided to take the worst of the garbage and put it into closed bins to keep the racoons out and went to bed.

I was preparing to go out in the bay with Dave. He'd put a couple of crab traps out and wanted to catch catfish for bait and to take out any crabs he'd caught. He also wanted to show me where the traps were so I could watch them. He was leaving this morning and wouldn't be back for awhile.

It's best to leave the traps in the water, but they should be checked, daily, so crabs don't get inside and die. They start killing each other when they run out of bait. That draws more of them.

We had cleaned up the aftermath of the party and disposed of all the garbage. It was dead low tide when we got up and winter lows are *very* low in Estero Bay, so we waited until around nine o'clock to go out, because the channel is almost dry in the bay on those low tides.

Alma called to tell me to get the phone. I picked up the

one nearby in the potting shed.

"Mr. Grimes? This is Selma Wentworth. I met you last evening at your party."

"I remember you very well, Selma. I steadfastly refuse liability for hangovers! – and call me CD."

"Thanks, CD. You can't have forgotten Bonnie Patrick. I'm afraid there's some real trouble now."

"Did she run off with another husband?"

"She won't be running off with anyone, anymore. They just opened the pool here at the court and she was laying there – dead. She was murdered sometime last night or this morning.

"Alma said you're a detective and I think I remember reading something about you in the papers. I think maybe you could be needed in this mess.

"It was bound to happen, sooner or later. Now a lot of people who were at your party will be suspects, unless there's something to point to one person.

"CD, we didn't like her, at all, but she was more pathetic than anything else. I don't think any of us would actually kill her.

"Will you come?"

"What do the police say about it, so far?"

"They aren't here yet. I live two trailers down from the pool and ran over here when I heard Mrs. Bellows screaming. I called the police and, now, you. She found her at nine o'clock. It's only nine oh four now."

"How do you know it was murder?"

"Because her head has a big bruise on it right over her left eye and a towel is tied in a knot around her throat."

"Don't touch anything. I'll be right there."

I yelled to Dave that Bonnie Patrick had been murdered

last night, thanked him (facetiously) for predicting it, and jumped in the old Jeep. I was at the trailer court in less than three minutes. A sheriff's car was pulling up as I got out of the Jeep and we went in together.

Selma was in the reception room with a woman in her mid-sixties who she introduced as Mrs. Bellows. She pointed to the door to the pool area.

"She's over by the ladies' changing room door is why no one saw her," Selma explained. "We don't know how she got in."

I went out with the deputy, who introduced himself as Sgt. Dan Ford. He stopped short as soon as we saw the body, and exclaimed, "It's Bonnie!"

"They didn't tell you who she was when they called?"

"Yeah, but I never knew her last name before. I, er, I met her in a place, uh...."

"So did about everyone else around these parts, if what they tell me is true. She's wearing a bathing suit, so she's been in the changing room, I suppose. I guess that means she was meeting her killer here by appointment – or maybe she met the guy's wife, instead."

She was laying behind a row of deck chairs where she couldn't be seen from the outside through the chain link fence around the area. There were six strands of barbed wire on top of the fence on triangular shaped stanchions. She got in either through the gate or through the building.

I bent over and looked closely at her body, not touching anything. Dan started to say something, then shrugged and asked if I was the one who was a special marshal for the grand jury or something. He'd read about it in the papers.

"I'm a special officer for Sheriff Len Stewart's department and for the state, at times. I'm mostly used as an expert witness, but I was given investigative powers when I handled that bit with Senator Edgerton."

"That's where I read the stuff. I was glad somebody finally got that lousy rotten bastard! You should get the citizenship medal!"

I saw what Selma meant about the big bruise over her eye. The towel was knotted so tightly it was cutting into the flesh.

"I'd say she was laying on that lounge chair and someone came along from this side and hit her with something. She was stunned or probably unconscious and they tied the bath towel around her throat and yanked it tight, dragging her off the chair. Then they dropped her and took something out of her little pocket there, then left. What was in her suit pocket was probably the key to that gate, so we'd better be damned sure to get any prints before anyone starts messing around with the padlock. I'd say she's been dead about four or five hours, but I'm not an expert on that.

"It could have been a man or a woman. She was stunned, so didn't resist.

"I want to see in the dressing room."

The police lab truck pulled up out front as I headed into the dressing room. I wanted a look before they came in to tell me to get the hell out. I made it a point to not touch anything except the edge of the door, very high, and with a handkerchief. There were no wet footprints or anything such to be seen, but I was careful not to touch anything. Dan followed closely, watching my every move.

"Lights were left on in here. May be important. That's the dress she was wearing at the party last night, there. Someone went through it and through her purse. She had something they wanted.

"Do you know how she made her living?"

"Uh, no. I only talked to her a couple of times."

I didn't touch anything in the basket of clothes, but I looked it over, carefully. The clothes were left rumpled and the purse's contents were dumped on top of them.

I then looked quickly around the long narrow room, but it was spotless. There wasn't any cigarette butt or anything else to give a clue.

I went back outside to be greeted by Lt. Sam Lukens, homicide detective. We'd worked together on a couple of other cases, so he knew me and didn't raise hell with Dan for letting me nose around. He knew I was more careful than his own officers.

"What we got?" Sam asked.

"What you see is what you get," Dan reported. "There aren't any clues that're too obvious in there. Somebody searched her clothes and purse and Mr. Grimes noted the turned-out little pocket on her suit, so she probably had the key to the gate in there.

"She was at a party last night. Mr. Grimes was there."

"It was at my house. She left about eleven o'clock. Alone.

"It's good you notice such little things, Dan. They can be important."

"Anybody at the party express any dislike for her?" Sam asked.

"Well, only a hundred people or so," Selma said, coming out of the reception office. "Bonnie wasn't popular with women. Particularly married women. She was a bit fond of husbands.

"I called CD to come as soon as I called you. He had a lot of suspects at his house last night. She even managed to get Mac to threaten her in public, but about fifty people have done that."

"She was threatened?" Sam asked.

"Mac McMullins threatened to tie her tits in a knot for her if she tried to screw up his son, Sean's, marriage," I answered. "I understand she was used to at least one threat a week or she wasn't happy. My wife told the other women how to handle her type. She got discouraged and left early."

"Yeah! She probably saw your wife was going to be far too much competition," Sam said. "I can deduce she was the kind who likes to play all the women against each other and against herself so she's the center of attention?"

"Seemed like that. It was what I thought as soon as she drooled all over me with Alma standing right there."

"The sexy bathing suit says that," Sam countered. "She worked hard to keep that figure and she showed it off. I find a woman wears something like that for only one purpose. To make the other women jealous. If they have the body for it, they don't need a skimpy bathing suit to advertise it."

"That's how Alma got rid of her," Selma said. "She told us to not let any jealousy show at all, and to even act like we could stand her. She didn't know what else to do, so she left."

"OK. Who had the most recent motive?" Sam asked.

"You'll have to find which husbands she was entertaining last week," Selma said. "Bill Kocsis was the last one I knew about, but that could be old news, with her. It *was* two or three weeks ago."

The lab equipment came in and they spent the next hour going over the place. The padlock was wiped clean and there was no indication they had been anywhere except in the fenced area and in the changing room. Sam asked Mrs. Bellows a few questions, then let Selma take her home.

"I don't think we're going to get much cooperation from any of the women on this one," Dan said with a grin, after they left. "Bonnie was a lot of things, but greatly loved by her peers and neighbors wasn't one of them."

"I want to go to her trailer to look around, but I think one of you should go with me. I think I'll have to be very careful with this one."

"What does that mean?" Sam asked.

"These women all felt threatened by Bonnie. They think no man could be unmoved by her sexuality. She was throwing herself at me last night until Alma made a joke of it. I think maybe our sexy little Bonnie wasn't above a bit of blackmail. If she had the key in that pocket, why go through her clothes and purse?"

"You think she was meeting someone to put the vice on?" Dan asked.

"I don't really know. I'll want to know a lot about her before I come to any conclusions, but that bathing suit cost plenty and the clothes she wore didn't come from K-Mart. That purse has eighteen karat gold thread woven through it and cost over a thousand bucks. I know, because I got one for Alma, but not so flashy.

"I think there's a lot about that one we have to learn."

"I sent a car to her place when we came in," Sam said. "We've done what we can here, for now, so let's go see what the little lady had at home."

He left Dan in charge of the murder scene and we went the two blocks to Bonnie's trailer. Her Thunderbird was sitting in the carport with the keys in the console tray.

"Want to bet on whether we're the first to want to look

around the house?"

"She drove to the clubhouse and her killer drove back here and went inside, throwing the keys back into the console tray. Otherwise, the keys would be in her purse. If they were in the trailer we might believe she left them there and walked, but nobody leaves the keys to a new car in the car. Not even if she were drunk or left it in her own garage or something."

We went on inside with her keys while the lab man sprinkled dust on the steering wheel. I could see right away the killer had worn gloves. There wasn't anything showing in the dust. Not even old prints from Bonnie.

The trailer had been searched, but very quickly. Whoever did the searching didn't know how. Sam put the lab boys onto listing everything and we went back outside.

Bonnie's trailer was on a corner across from a little park area, so there was no trailer across or to our right as we faced it. The trailer to the left was a neat green and white job. Kitty Lorris saw me and came out to ask what was going on.

"I'm afraid Bonnie was murdered sometime this morning. Her body's at the clubhouse. Did you see or hear anything out of the ordinary?"

"Well, she was always coming and going. We didn't pay any attention, and we *did* have enough to drink so we wouldn't...," Kitty began, then, "You say her body was at the clubhouse? Then why is her car here?"

"Do you know what time the car came back?" Sam asked.

"Well, something did wake me up. It was around three o'clock. I don't know if I heard her car coming in or something else. I looked at the clock and it.... It was her car coming in, because I remember wondering if she'd brought somebody home with her. I remember because I knew the bars closed at two, so it was a sort of strange time for her to be coming in.

"It was three ten. We have that digital clock with the red numbers that shows from anywhere all over the room. I looked at it and thought it a strange time, even for her."

"Chances are, it wasn't her. Try to remember. Was there anything else? Anything at all?"

"Wasn't her? Oh, dear! It was her *killer*?! That's why her car wasn't there with her – because her *killer* brought it back? Oh, dear!"

"The killer was looking for something in her trailer," Sam told her. "Did you see or hear anything else, at all? Anything at all might be important."

"No, I went back to sleep. Bat doesn't ever wake up for anything.

"Oh, dear!"

"Well, there's no danger now," Sam assured her. "He's come and gone. You can bet he won't be back around here again."

We went back inside and methodically went through the trailer. There was a small wall safe behind a picture (How very original!) with the combination the birth date on her driver's license. The police always try that sort of thing on the types of safes where the owner selects and sets his own combination. It works, most of the time. The number will be a birth date, social security numbers or something like that.

There were jewels and cash worth about thirty grand in the safe, along with some old coins, deeds and titles and home insurance papers, but that was about all – except for a key to a safe deposit box and a receipt for rental from a local bank.

"I'd say any blackmail evidence would be in that box," Sam said. "I can't have you in on that, but I'll let you know what we find, strictly off the record. I can't go too far, but this kind of thing's usually easier for someone like you than it is for us. We don't have the time or manpower to spend on a case where half the county would like to see the victim dead."

I thanked him for letting me tag along, so far, and went back out and over to Selma's trailer. She fixed coffee and a grilled ham and cheese sandwich and sat to talk.

"I'll tell you a lot about what I know. I can tell you from the start that a good bit of it will be stuff I heard or stuff that's mostly gossip. I can tell you that when I couldn't tell the police, because you'll know how to handle it without running around accusing anybody of anything.

"You ask the questions. I'll try to answer."

"The police are going to want to know where you were at ten after three this morning. That's a few minutes after she was killed, but it's a time when we know where the killer was."

"I was here, in bed, all alone. Where was he?"

"He drove her car back to her trailer and went in to try to find something. It woke Kitty Lorris up when he drove in at three ten. She remembered the time because it was strange, even for Bonnie.

"Tell me about Kitty and Bat Lorris."

"Let's see. They're next door to her place, aren't they? I don't know them at all well. I see Kitty at the clubhouse, sometimes. She plays bridge. Bat plays golf and has some kind of job with a construction company. I think he's a carpenter. Kitty doesn't feel threatened by Bonnie. She says living right next door gives her some protection, because that's much too close for comfort.

"She gets along with everybody. I doubt either of them would want to kill her."

"She had an affair with Bill Kocsis?"

"Let's see. That was about four weeks ago, when Betty went to Detroit to see her folks. She hadn't been gone two hours before Bonnie moved in on Bill.

"Now, this is mostly what I heard from Pat Schultz, who lives across from Bill and Betty, so it's probably about half true. Just bear that in mind.

"Pat said Bill got back from taking Betty to the airport and decided to mow the lawn or something out front like that. Bonnie drove up and started telling him how she wished she had a big strong man like him to mow her place, because it was just *too much* for po' l'il ol' her!

"To make a long story shorter Bill started going over to her place to mow the lawn for her, but it seemed to take him hours, and you know the size of these places. I have seven and a half feet of grass on the sides and back and six feet in front to the sidewalk – and the lots are all alike.

"Betty was gone five days and Bill mowed the lawn for Bonnie five times and went to do the trimming or something at night. I think everybody here knows all about it except Betty, who sure as hell has her suspicions. She asked me what I knew and I told her I didn't *know* anything and wouldn't spread gossip, but to remember there were always rumors and not all of them were true.

"I think she decided it wasn't worth the trouble to face Bill with it. Sleeping with a nymphomaniac tramp like that doesn't mean anything to a man. Her big worry is that Bill would catch something and give it to her. You mentioned AIDS and herpes last night, if you remember.

"I know part of it has to be true, because it's stuff Pat saw and heard directly, not something somebody told her. I don't think Pat would lie about anything like that."

"What part did she hear and see personally?"

"Well, she'd been to Naples for some of her charity work, but got sick from some bad shrimp and came home. She got there about when Bonnie started the `Oh, poor li'l ol' me!' routine on Bill. Pat said she came home just as Bonnie got out of her car and went over to drape herself all over Bill's mower. She said Bonnie had parked right in front of her mailbox and she had trouble getting her car into the drive because it was so close. She could hear it all. Norm was inside, taking a nap, and came out to help carry and heard part of it. He said Bonnie sure worked fast, and Pat asked what he meant. He told Pat about Bill having taken Betty to the airport only a couple of hours ago and Bonnie descending on him before poor Betty was even comfortable in her seat. Pat said she kidded Norm about Bonnie. Norm said he had better ways to spend his time and he could do better at any bar.

"He and Pat kid that way all the time. They both saw Bill load his mower in his station wagon and take off after her. I think Jim Tooney was sort of spending a lot of time at her place at the time and had been doing her mowing and trimming and that sort of thing himself, then Bill moved in and they've been arguing about it ever since. I know they used to talk a lot and even used to go fishing together all the time and now they don't even speak to each other. That's the sad thing about that kind of woman. It's not enough she causes trouble between a man and his wife she also has to cause trouble among friends. It was inevitable that somebody'd kill her sooner or later. She was asking for it all the time.

"That's the daytime drama story of Bill and Betty Kocsis and the ever lovin' – in the physical sense – Bonnie Patrick."

Chapter two

"As long as we're so close to the subject, tell me about Jim Tooney," I said. "My author friend saw Bill Kocsis and Jim having a yelling match out in the bay yesterday and you mentioned him and how Bonnie seems to have broken up a long friendship between them."

"There's not much there," Selma answered. "Jim's been going with Bonnie for a long time, but she wasn't much interested in him. He's single, which took all the fun out of it, for her.

"Jim's from New Jersey. He works for the City of Fort Myers on the highway department. He's foreman of a crew. He's been down here for a bit more than eight years. I've dated him once or twice. He's a fairly nice guy, but a bit too chauvinistic, for my tastes. He tries to own you. I don't like that. I can't be confined that way.

"He was friends with Steve Keene until Bonnie had her little fling with him, then they stopped having anything to do with each other.

"Sean McMullin never was what you could call his friend, so there wasn't anything lost when she went after him, even though I don't really think she.... Mostly, she used husbands to make Jim jealous.

"I don't know how long he'll stay mad at Bill, but Jim will find another woman like Bonnie. That's the type he wants. I guess he knows there's no danger of him ever ending up married to one of those, deep inside. He's really scared of marriage. He's not much on commitment. I don't think he'd kill her, but I can't see how any of us could — and one of us did!"

"I'm just looking for some background. Usually murder of this type is the result of several things. So far, I have Bill being dumped and Jim being jealous. Bill's married, so I don't see that as motive, unless she was going to cause problems between Bill and Betty. You said Betty wouldn't react all that strongly to the thing because she understands a woman like Bonnie doesn't really mean anything but a good time to a man. You've said enough about Betty that I also put her as a secondary suspect. She said her piece to Bonnie and was ready to chalk the experience up as part of the past.

"You seem to think Jim wouldn't kill her, but I can see one or two reasons he might. He's a primary suspect until something better comes along or until he has a good enough alibi."

"You can see good reasons why he'd kill her?"

"If the autopsy shows she was pregnant? If she was blackmailing him? You said yourself he wasn't the marrying kind. If she was pregnant she might have been pressuring him. Anyone would kill over blackmail if pushed too far, and the killer was certainly looking for *some*thing in her trailer and in that dressing room!

"You mentioned Steve Keene had an affair? Tell me about him and his wife."

"Steve's from New York – upstate somewhere. He works for the Imperial Yacht Sales outlet on old forty one. He's their general sales manager, I think. He's been here three years.

"Helen works at the Bonita Shopper's News as a copy girl and general gofer. She writes that column about food and has her own byline, now and then. They both have good senses of humor. They're just like they seemed to be at your party. They laugh a lot and do have a lot of fun. Everybody likes them. They don't take others too seriously and don't expect to be taken seriously, in turn.

"Bonnie met him at the clubhouse and she asked him to teach her to play pinochle. Before long they were playing house at her place evenings when Helen was getting the paper ready for the press. It comes out every Thursday, so usually Wednesday nights and fairly often Tuesday nights she's working until all hours.

"I think Helen knew all about it from the first. Bonnie did little things to let her know, so Helen finally told her – at the clubhouse where everyone could hear – that she could play house all she wanted, so long as he was there to keep their own place fixed up and so long as he paid all the bills on time. She said if Steve caught any whore disease and brought it home to her she would be right over to discuss the burial arrangements for the two of them.

"That seemed to end it for Bonnie. Helen wasn't going to make a big deal out of it and she wasn't going to get all jealous and mad, so there wasn't any point to continuing the affair. She just stopped seeing Steve. Bonnie needed the hatred of the wife to add spice to her affairs. Steve used to laugh about it and say Helen had better sense than to get mad about some easy lay. It was no big deal he slept with her because there probably weren't ten men in the park who *hadn't* had her. It was sort of the expected thing to do. He would laugh and say he only wanted to be one of the group, so, if he had to bong her, he had to bong her.

"That wasn't the way either of them really felt, but it was a very effective way to end the thing in a civilized manner.

"Steve's friendly enough with her, but Helen never did have anything to do with her, and that didn't change. The only one who got mad about it was Jim, but he was about over it.

"That's a bit too liberal and open for my own tastes. I'd have to dump the guy for awhile until we had a solid understanding about exactly how far each of us could go with someone else and get away with it.

"I don't think Helen or Steve had anything to do with killing the bitch. It simply wasn't the kind of thing they would see as necessary. Helen won that little war, hands down, and there was nothing left she could have blackmailed Steve about."

"Do – did – these guys often buy her presents?"

"Well, I don't really know. I guess they would, but nothing big. She always had more money than she knew what to do with."

"But no one knows where she got it."

"That's true. I think Connie would probably know. Connie's some relation to her. I guess it could be blackmail, but she had the money when she got here. She could've been blackmailing people where she came from, so that doesn't explain anything, does it?"

"What do you know about her, other than what I've learned last night and today? I can guess a lot, but I have to know how she lived and about her finances."

"She came down here a little over six years ago from Baltimore. She bought her place for cash, moved in – and moved in – if you get me. She always said she was an artist, but no one ever saw anything she was supposed to have done except a couple of little paintings she donated to one of the first charity auctions we had. They WERE good. She made a little statue or two that were good. Maybe more than good, actually. I have to grudgingly admit that.

"I guess she did have a lot of talent, but I don't think she ever worked at it – I wasn't invited into her home to view any art – or anything else. I doubt any woman in the area has been invited to her place.

"Other than that, you know everything I do, in general. All I can do is give a few details and a lot of idle gossip, but I've checked out a lot of the gossip and it's all been true, so far."

"What about Connie?"

"Connie's nice. She's divorced. She moved in here five years ago with her husband, but hubby left again within six months. He claimed he couldn't find decent employment here and hated the place. She said she liked the place and hated him. He pays her alimony and she has some money of her own invested. She says the marriage was really over for a couple of years before they moved here. She didn't let it bother her much that he was gone.

"Connie dates a bit, but she doesn't want to get serious with anyone. She likes to fish and she's good on the organ and piano. She's got a good voice, in a bland sort of way, and plays Friday and Saturday nights at a small nightclub on the beach.

"Connie's comfortable. She's well-liked here and at her work. She didn't have anything to do with the killing."

"You told me she was part of the group who wouldn't speak to Bonnie."

"She was only related to Bonnie, not a friend."

"Hm. Could Bonnie have had anything to do with the hubby's leaving so soon?"

"No. Bonnie was here! If there was anything to that he would have stayed. Connie knew what Bonnie was because they knew each other all their lives, so she steered clear. It was that simple.

"You can talk to her about Bonnie. She lives straight over on the next block. The tan, yellow and white double trailer with the pink alamandas all over the carport stanchions. It's Monday, so she'll be home until three, then she'll go over to work at the Audubon Society."

"It's after one thirty, so I'll go there now. Can I come back and get the rest of the background?"

"Sure! I'll go with you to Connie's, if you want, then we can come back here and I'll make us something to snack on. I snack a lot and don't eat any large meals."

We walked over to Connie's and were invited to come in. Selma explained what I wanted.

"I heard about the murder. I guess she asked for it long and hard enough. I'm surprised somebody didn't kill her a lot of years ago.

"I don't know a lot about her, lately, other than local gossip. What do you want to know?"

"Basically, how she made her living. She had a lot of very expensive things, but no visible means of support, so far as I can tell. She said she was an artist, but I haven't seen any evidence of her work around and I don't know the name."

"She sells her art work under the name of Bonnie Bond. She has a show every three years. It was her one talent where she really *was* good."

"I didn't think she painted that much," Selma said. "I only saw those two little pieces she sold at the auction."

"She exhibited thirty or so paintings every three years and got anywhere from four thousand to fifteen thousand a painting," Connie said. "Maharashahzi's Gallery in New

York. I helped her with one show seven or eight years ago. She exhibited thirty pieces and sold them all. Before the fees and so forth, she raked in one hundred eighty three thousand six hundred fifteen dollars! She had a lot more money than she knew what to do with.

"I know everyone thinks she was blackmailing people, and I really should have told you how she made her money, but I really didn't care to stop any gossip about her. She was a total bitch to me all our lives.

"We were raised a few blocks apart. She was a second cousin.

"I thought she had grown up and had a change of heart when she asked me to help with the show. She was very nice until the day it opened, then she had the nerve to say the show was a big success despite how much I tried to sabotage her and make her look bad.

"She was just trying to get Earl away from me, but he didn't come around the show and she didn't have any use for me, except for Earl.

"Hell! She could have had him with my blessings! The scuzz was already running around with that airhead at the restaurant. He didn't really have any time for Bonnie.

"She paid me exactly one hundred dollars to go into New York every day, ten to twelve hours a day, for five days. She seemed to resent having to pay me, at all.

"I guess you'll want to know where I was when she was killed, after all that, so when was it?"

"Around three this morning."

"I was with a gentleman friend, Buck Finley. When I left your party, I was a little drunk – you know that. You had Steve and Helen take me home because Norm was a bit too drunk to drive and I came with him and Pat. Steve took us all three.

"Buck came in about then– he lives across over there on a diagonal – number thirteen twenty two. Anyway, he was fixing to go out for ladyfish. It's full moon enough that they're hitting pretty good, so we went out and got back about four thirty, then we had some breakfast and went to bed. We caught some fish, but you know we don't keep them."

"Well! That will mean you two're the only ones we can absolutely eliminate as a suspect, so far!" Selma said. "The rest of us went home alone or with spouses."

"Hah! You can eliminate Pat and Norm! I think they might still be passed out! I had to help Steve and Helen get them inside. Steve sorta dumped Norm on the couch and Helen and I got Pat undressed and into bed. They're not used to drinking. They're really going to be suffering today, I'll bet!"

We talked a bit more, then went back to Selma's place.

"I didn't think anyone got actually falling-down drunk at my party. I tried to watch the guests. I guess Norm and Pat just can't hold their liquor well."

"Not many of us are used to it, here. I have to watch how much I drink, but I guess Norm and Pat didn't use any sense. I know Pat drank a lot because I tried to slow her down. Norm had a glass in his hand every time I looked at him.

"At least you know who not to invite to booze parties anymore. Norm, Pat, and Connie drink too much, and Karl and Edna Forbes are strict teetotalers who should have better sense than to accept an invitation to a New Year's party anywhere but at their church."

"You said Karl and Edna were among your private little

not-speaking-to-Bonnie group. I noticed they were a bit stiff and formal last night, almost insultingly so.

"Reformed alcoholics?"

"No. They're religious fanatics, really. They're the born-again types who make a career of telling everyone else how to live the perfect life. If it even makes you smile it's a sin and it's wrong! I doubt they've ever tasted anything with alcohol in it. Not even cough syrup. To taste the evil stuff will send them straight to hell, don't pass go and don't collect two hundred dollars!

"You can bet they believe with all their little narrow minds that everyone at your party is doomed for eternity. You can bet neither of them had anything to do with the killing."

"Uh-oh! That type will kill in a second if they feel they have a call from god. There's no way they could have missed the fact Bonnie was sin incarnate!"

"And then searched her and her trailer? I doubt it. It wouldn't make any sense."

"It would, in one way. If he had his own fling with her?"

"I could see Bonnie taking his attitude as a challenge, but I can't picture her going after such as him. You had to notice the sour, pinched looks on their faces. I don't think he's capable of being stimulated enough to make it with any woman. I'd be willing to bet those two haven't had sex in years. They had one kid, a daughter, who ran away from home two years ago, when she was sixteen. They wouldn't have had sex except to have children, and they had the one they wanted."

"You're probably right, but I think I want to know a good bit more about them. What about Norm and Pat?"

"They live across the street from Bill and Betty. We've

really covered them already. They were too drunk to have done it. Connie wouldn't lie about that, and you *did* make them let Steve and Helen drive them home. The only thing I can add is that Norm is the general caretaker of the trailer court here and that Pat manages the business office. They get rent and utilities for Pat's part and Norm makes enough extra to get by on with the caretaking. They both have plenty of spare time, but they have CD's and some other minor investments. They go out with lots of other people at various times. They're well-liked."

"I saw Dave Weitz talking to Bonnie last night, then his wife came over, grabbed his arm, nodded at her, gave her a look that could fry eggs, and marched Dave off. What about them?"

"Dave's into general real estate. Sylvia is his secretary, receptionist, and a licensed dealer, herself. They do pretty well. Dave was from somewhere out west and Sylvia is from Orlando. They met on some land deal near Disney World, fell in love, and got married. They moved here two years ago when Harry Gottlieb died and Phyllis sold their trailer and moved back to Ontario.

"People seem to like them. I don't know them well, at all."

"You know a hell of a lot about all of these people,. Why?"

"I write the blurbs about the people in the park for the big newspapers in Naples and Fort Myers. Every time anything at all happens, they tell me about it. I know about a lot of things that could never be printed in any newspaper! You'd be very surprised to know some of the things a person will tell about someone else if they want to get at them."

"No, I definitely wouldn't! Remember, I'm a private detective who specializes in murder cases!

"OK. What about Bat and Kitty Lorris? They live next door to Bonnie's trailer."

"We've covered them in other ways. It's like I said, they're too close to be bothered by her. They're out. That makes them, Norm and Pat, the Forbes prudes, and Connie. We're making progress!"

"I won't go quite that far, yet. I have to investigate people like Karl and Edna Forbes very carefully. I don't trust any fanatic in any way, any time, about anything. I can't help it. I do *not* like those two.

"What about Tom and Jean Billings? She was in that bunch who wanted to get Bonnie aside and beat hell out of her."

"They've only been here for about four months or less. I don't know too much about them. They're from Maryland. They're renting the trailer while Tom works on the engineering of the new sewer plant, then they'll go back home. They're quiet and don't mix with others much."

"Mac McMullins is my obvious choice, but I tend to think he's innocent. He'd smack her around a bit, but he wouldn't kill her. Tell me about him."

"Oh, Mac's our local character," she said with a laugh. "He's a radical about a lot of things, on the surface, but it's just the way people see him. His views are middle of the road. He goes in too strongly for causes. I get a kick out of it and like his crazy sense of humor. It's sort of weird. I'm attracted to people with weird ideas, I think. They're usually rather intelligent."

"My friend, Dave, the author, is like that. What about him and his son and daughter-in-law?"

"They're from Tennessee. Mac moved in here when the court opened nine years ago and bought four lots. They're back by the canal. He put his trailer across two lots and bought the double wide Sean and Lorna live in to put next door. Sean and Lorna moved in a year later. Mac's a mullet fisherman, but he's not one of those who cause all the trouble. He says he'd support a law making it illegal to use a gill net within a hundred feet of any seawall, embankment or shore. If something's not worked out pretty soon there's going to be trouble about the commercial netters. That's the biggest gripe against them around here – they come in late at night and race around dropping their nets in the boat channels. That washes the banks down anywhere there aren't good sea walls and beats the boats against the docks and walls.

"None of the channels are more than a hundred fifty feet wide, so the rule would put an end to gill nets in the channels. They passed that law in one county – I think it was up in Pinellas County. It almost put the netters out of business.

"He says another way to handle that is like they did in Hernando County. Make it illegal to strike the nets with the motor in the water. That way, they can't wash the banks or do any damage with their wake.

"He's in a lot of controversy most of the time because of that sort of thing, but he claims a few of the netters who are born assholes are ruining the business for all of them and he'd like to see them stopped cold while there still *is* a business.

"Sean and Lorna also run mullet boats and they have some crab traps out in the bay. They keep to themselves unless someone else makes the first move, then they're as good a friend as you can have. They're the type who'll very literally give you their last scrap of food, if you need it. I refuse to believe they'd have anything to do with killing Bonnie. Sean is the only married man I ever went after, but he turned me down. He did it in such a way that I felt good about it, if you can believe. We're all good friends now. I told Lorna I went after her man and she said she didn't blame me. She doesn't see how any woman could resist him.

"Bonnie went after him too, but she wouldn't give it up when he turned her down, so Mac speaks his mind about her and to her every time they're anywhere around each other. There was never any danger of her coming between Sean and Lorna, but Mac thinks she should be a bit more discreet. Apparently, it's OK if the man fools around, but it's some kind of great shame if the wife finds out about it in a way that humiliates her publicly."

"I was born and raised in that kind of place. I know exactly what you're saying. It's expected that the man will find a piece on the side, now and then, but it's not acceptable to place the wife into a position where she would have to admit that it could happen with her own husband. It's not what you do so much as it's what other people know about.

"The only other person who fits into this mess I know about is Jennie Allen. Tell me about her."

"She's Paul's mother. She owns the place where they all live. Bonnie went after Paul, hard, when they moved in a year and a half ago, but Jennie broke it up before it started. She calmly told Bonnie she'd cut.... She told her to back off a few miles and stay backed off. She meant it, so Bonnie backed off. She's a feisty one.

"Paul works for an appliance distributorship. He likes to play golf and Winnie likes tennis. They spend a lot of their time at one of the clubs. They're members of several, I think. I don't think any of them are likely. I can't see how they would be."

"I agree. With the blackmail angle out, I don't see where this case connects. The killer was looking for *some*thing! He took a hell of a chance going to her place to search."

"Who do you still have as suspects?"

"Well, there's you," I said with a grin. "There's Bill and Betty, together or separate. Jim, Steve and Helen, Karl and Edna – or just Karl. I think Edna is out. She's the poisoner type. If there'd been poison I'd be on her like water on a lake! Norm and Pat aren't completely out of it, and Tom and Jean.

"I don't think you did it. I wouldn't be here talking to you, if I did, but it's still quite a long list. It could be someone I don't know about yet, but I don't think that's likely."

"I don't see why Tom and Jean Billings are in it."

"Because they're from Maryland and are here temporarily? Bonnie was from Maryland? I have to find out about some things in Maryland before I consider dropping them from my list."

"I see. Norm and Pat?"

"Primarily, because it's too easy to fake being drunk. I think Pat's definitely out. You *saw* her drinking, but I never did actually see Norm take a swallow. He always had a glass in his hand and he refilled it often enough, but I didn't see him drink it.

"Jim's in, because he's the obvious suspect. If it turns out she was pregnant he'll be it. He might have let jealousy get to him. The rest are obvious suspects. Men who had affairs and their wives who would resent such a woman."

We talked a bit longer, then I said I'd want to call on the others while I was still in the trailer court and left. Selma marked a map for me to everyone's property.

I talked to Jennie Allen, but Paul and Winnie were at work. She said they'd all come home at around two o'clock and no one had left before the two went to work at seven thirty. She knew no one went out because there was an alarm that woke her every time the gate opened.

I didn't point out that the three foot fence could almost be stepped over. I thanked her and went to the end of the road. Mac and Sean were out in their net boats, but Lorna made me a cup of strong dark coffee full of chicory and we talked.

They took two people they knew from over by Coconut Road home at just after two, then came home. She and Sean had gone out to the grass flats and didn't get back before four thirty or five. The tide would be too low in the morning, so they got it done before going to bed, then slept until about one o'clock, then Mac and Sean took the mullet boats out.

"Did you see anyone on the bay?" I asked, not expecting they had.

"Well, Connie and Buck were fishing on the flats out of Spring Creek. We waved at them, but I don't know if they recognized us."

"I'd hoped someone saw them. Connie said they were out there fishing at the time of the murder and your seeing them corroborates it. It gives you and Sean a solid alibi, too, come to think of it!"

"Well, if we need one, I guess. I don't see why anyone

would think we'd kill her that way. If I thought her kind of white trash was worth killing I might take a sharp filleting knife to her. Sean would never hurt a woman, much less kill her.

"I guess Pops is why you suspect one of us, but Pops would probably take a horsewhip to her if he was that mad. I wasn't worried about her and Sean because he would never tumble to any cheap whore. If he needed another woman she'd be respectable and nobody'd even know anything about it. I can tell you he don't need anybody else.

"I know all the other women around here are always letting him know they're available, but that's just to be expected with a man like Sean. I can see you're a lot like him. You have to know how it is to have lovesick women chasing after you all the time. I imagine you and Sean do exactly the same thing – you tell them you're not looking, but you'll sure as hell look them up if you ever start looking because they're very special people and all that kind of crap. Make them feel good while letting them know there's no chance. I imagine Sean would even be that way with a cheap whore like Bonnie, but you wouldn't. You'd tell her you respected your woman too much to ever even look at everybody's girl.

"I think you know what I'm saying."

"Alma handled that for me last night."

"I saw that. Excuse me for saying this, but she's the kind of woman I would be afraid of if she didn't have someone like you. Sean would probably take her up if she even hinted she might be willing. You and me, we wouldn't ever know a thing about it. I'm glad you're man enough for her and you can be glad I'm woman enough to handle Sean. I think Alma and I will become good friends. I'm also glad you're a lot like Sean, too – because, if you wanted me, I don't honestly know what I'd do.

"You can see I trust you and I know you're decent or I'd never let you know that! I think maybe your family and mine will be close. I know Pops likes that friend of yours who writes those books. They were talking about all kinds of things. Pops gets wild hairs and goes off making the bigwigs hate his guts, but we sort of get a kick out of it."

We talked for awhile, then I went to call on the Forbes.

She was right, I think. We'll become good friends. I could see how Selma thought a lot of Sean for the way he turned her down and I had to admit I felt good because of the way Lorna said she could go for me. She actually made it impossible for me to ever make a pass while she said she would probably take me up on it!

Edna Forbes came to the door and actually sniffed when she saw who it was. She stood squarely in the way to be sure I didn't try to get inside.

"I'm CD Grimes. We met briefly at my place last evening. Miss Bonnie Patrick was murdered this morning, in case you haven't heard. I'm investigating her death."

"Hmpfth! My husband and I were at that awful drunken orgy! We found it disgusting! People like that trollop invite retribution by their acts! We are not concerned in any way in any part of it and don't wish to become involved! You go straight home and pray for your immortal soul's forgiveness! You spread the evil of strong drink like a plague in this community with your wild orgies! You will answer to a higher power!"

Karl came up behind her with the Bible in his hand. He looked down his nose at me and asked her what I wanted.

"You two are prime suspects in a murder investigation. I want to ask a couple of questions."

He dropped the Bible.

"You can either answer questions, here and now, or I can suggest to the sheriff he take you to the courthouse and question you, formally. Exactly how far does your religion extend?"

"Buh ... buh!" he blubbered, while she swayed around like she was about to faint. He wasn't where he could catch her, so she managed to hang onto the door frame until her lightheadedness passed.

"It's well known among the community that you two believe in death to anyone who doesn't see your moral views exactly like you do. Does that extend to you becoming the agents of the lord in such matters?

"Think very carefully before you answer me. Remember, there's also a commandment about false testimony. You could consign your own immortal souls to hell if you lie to me!"

"You get out of here! May the Lord curse your house! Get out!"

"OK. I'll leave. You can expect Detective Lukens to come haul you off in his police car. That should make a good impression on your evil neighbors.

"By the way, no one got particularly drunk, except for a few who chose to over-imbibe a bit, and we made sure they were safe and secure and that they didn't drive. The only orgy I noted was the two of you wallowing in your own personal orgy of judgment and condemnation of your neighbors. I think there's a decree in that Bible you're mopping the floor with there about what happens to those who dare to take the Lord's judgments onto themselves.

"Good day!"

He looked shocked, picked up the Bible and wiped it with his handkerchief. She was wide-eyed as I strolled off.

They probably didn't have anything to do with the murder, but I really could learn to totally despise such as those two. They judged everyone around themselves to a standard that was against all human nature and couldn't see they were, themselves, a long way from what their own church promoted.

Well, *she* didn't kill her, but *he* very well might have! If Bonnie had decided to see exactly how far he would go to preserve his phony sanctimonious piety and he caved in he wouldn't hesitate to kill her in moral indignation against the evil weakness of the flesh and for the destruction of the devil's tool. If she had a picture or something he would try to find it, at any risk. He could never live with any such thing around to show him up for what he was to the other fanatics he was bound to be a part of.

Steve and Helen Keene were home, so I stopped in. They offered me dinner and thanked me for a lovely evening the night before. They had gone with Dave and Sylvia Weitz to a beach party out on Bonita Beach to watch the sunrise on the first day of the year. They went directly from my party, so stayed together all night until sunrise at five fifty and a bit longer.

Four more people definitely out of the running for murderer.

"Did you see anyone else from my party there? Anyone else from the park?"

"Well, let me see. There were the Metzgers and the Adams and the Ripleys. There may have been a few others, but I didn't pay much attention."

I thanked them and left. My list of suspects was getting a bit shorter, so this was worthwhile for that.

I made one more stop. Norm Schultz was out in his front yard, so I stopped. My Jeep was still at Selma's and their place was on the way across the trailer court.

"How are you feeling today?"

"I'm fine. A bit headachey. I don't drink much and Pat doesn't either. She's in bad shape, but she admits she deserves it! I guess I do, too.

"Detective Lukens was here. He said you'd probably be around, but I'm afraid I don't remember enough to be of much help."

"I didn't think so. I only stopped because I'm on my way to Selma's to pick up my car and you were out here."

Pat came out to the front screened porch and waved, so I went over to sympathize for the way she was feeling.

"Oh, I know. I hope I didn't make a fool of myself last night. I'm not used to booze, but Norm kept pouring us more and, like a fool, I drank it. I was telling him we deserve how we feel today! Wouldn't it be nice if I could just die all at once and get it over with? My *hair* hurts! My *fingernails* hurt!"

We talked a minute, then I went on, got in my Jeep and went home, where Alma had a good supper waiting. I wrote down what I'd learned, then decided to forget the case until the next morning.

Chapter three

Dave had shown Alma where he put the crab traps, so she took me out in the morning to run them and put in new bait. She likes that kind of stuff and will handle the three traps herself when I'm not around.

Some of Dave's traps are kinda weird. A new design he's trying. He invents things.

We got six big males (Jimmies) and a lot of smaller ones and some females (Sooks), which we always release. She said she was going to catch some catfish for bait, later, if I wasn't home.

When I got back to the house I went over what I'd learned the day before and considered my list. I took several names off, then listed:

Karl Forbes = fanatic. Might have succumbed to her charms. She could have had a picture or something she was going to show around to shut the sanctimonious jerk up.

Mac McMullins = might have lost his temper and killed her, but I didn't believe it. I couldn't see any motive to him.

Paul and/or Winnie Allen = because they weren't eliminated. Motive?

Jennie Allen = ditto.

Norm Schultz = could have faked the drunk act. Motive? Pat WAS drunk so she was out.

Bill and/or Betty Kocsis = same as the Allens.

Tom and/or Jean Billings = find out about Maryland.

Jim Tooney = jealousy and she was making a fool out of him.

Selma Wentworth = She could have done it, but motive?

I didn't want Selma on that list. I liked her, but I'd learned, sadly, a very long time ago, not to let personal feelings affect my investigations.

That was the crop, at the moment. They all may have had the opportunity and the motive. I had started out yesterday with 22 suspects and had narrowed it to exactly half of that. If I could do as well today and continue that ratio I would solve the case in no more than five more days, on the outside. I had no intention of letting this take five more days. It should be possible to run everything down today and solve it by tomorrow. (If I was thinking any such trash I'd probably take a year. It doesn't work that way.)

I told Alma I was going, took the Jeep, and went over to the police station to talk with Sam Lukens. He might have eliminated someone else for me. He could find out things that happened elsewhere better than I could.

"You notice what we didn't find at her house when we looked yesterday?".

"No art supplies. I noticed that. She may have waited until a couple of months before her art exhibitions to paint anything, but she would have to have the supplies."

"I put a notice out for records to find if she or Bonnie Bond had some other place where she worked. She pays rent on a farm house out east of Lehigh Acres. It's in the middle of nowhere. It's in Southern Hendry County, but this is a murder investigation, so they'll expect me there. I called. I was just about to go out there to look around with my crew. You can come along, if you like.

"I found out one other thing that could prove important, or it could mean nothing, whatever. Maybe you can see why her art dealer would kill her?"

"If he had a bunch of her stuff and she died, the price

would really skyrocket – if she was as good as she seems to have been. I thought she was with some gallery in New York?"

"The representative, a guy by the name of Hensley, is supposed to be on his way here to gather the stuff for her exhibition on January twenty eighth to February second. We have to find him, if he's already here. The owner of the gallery said he was going to have Christmas with his own family in Virginia, then was coming down here to get the art stuff, then was going to take it all back. I had a notice sent out to all hotels and motels to locate Rochester Manson Hensley, representative of Maharashahzi's Art Galleries of New York.

"You want to drive your Jeep? I'll ride with you and can come back with the crew."

We went out to the Jeep and he told his crew to follow us. We could talk on channel fourteen on my CB if we had to. I headed out to I-75, then north to 82, having to cut back on 82, but them're the breaks.

"Did you learn anything else about any of our suspects?"

"Connie Peters and the McMullins were out in the bay when she was killed. The Keene, Weitz, Metzger and Ripley families are accounted for and all the Allens are out of it."

"I know about all but the Allens. Bat and Kitty Lorris are out of it, as far as I'm concerned."

"I never had them in it. The Allens were at their office. There was a break-in in the place next door and they were called at two twenty, went to the office and were with several members of the Naples police department until three fifteen or so. They didn't have time to get back to the trailer park and kill her. The old lady hadn't been out when they got back. They have an alarm thing they put on her door to wake her up if she sleepwalks. It was still in place."

"I didn't know about that. I talked some with Jennie. She said they hadn't gone out because she had a thing on the gate that would have let her know."

"They go out through the far side. They didn't want to wake her up at that hour, so they jumped the fence. They keep her car in the carport, but his is left outside the fence. It checks out."

"That leaves eight suspects – nine, so I'm right on schedule.

"Nine? I thought we had the whole county and New York!"

"No. I figure it was someone at my party. Selma says the serious threats were all there. She did something or said something to one of them there that ended up with her dead. The only other likely is that art dealer – and he may not have even been here yet."

I turned north on 29 and went to a little town called Felda, then turned back west just beyond it on a well-kept secondary agricultural road. We went several more miles, then Sam started watching the mailboxes. He told me to turn in at a dirt road to the north. About half a mile along it he pointed to an old farmhouse and said that was it.

We turned in and found a rented Buick sitting out front. Sam waved for the crew, who followed us in to surround the house and we went to the door and pushed it open. Sam had his revolver out, while I was staying behind him and close to the wall.

There were stacks of canvases in crates with code

numbers on them and the sharp sounds of hammering from the room to the side. We went to the door to find a thin young man sealing a crate. He looked up and squealed at the gun pointed at his head.

"Police! Freeze!" Sam yelled.

"What the hell?!" he cried. "Why...?! Who...?! What the hell!? I...! What the hell?!"

"Are you Rochester Hensley?" I asked.

"Yes! Who in the hell are you?! Are you out of your *minds*?"

"How long have you been here?" Sam asked.

"I just got here about half an hour ago! What *is* this?!"

"We mean when did you get to the area?" I asked.

"Sunday night. Why? What's going on? Who are you?"

"I'm Detective Sam Lukens, Homicide. This is CD Grimes, a state investigations expert.

"When did you see Miss Patrick last?"

"I don't know any Miss Patrick. What is this about?"

"Bonnie Bond's real name was Bonnie Patrick. She lived out near Spring Creek."

"Wait a minute! *Was* her name? She *lived*?"

"Yes. She was murdered at about three o'clock in the morning of the first. We just found out about this place. We heard about the show and that you were coming to get the art. We've been looking for you since early this morning."

"I'm staying at the Airport Inn. This is terrible!"

"I guess her art will really be worth a bundle now, right?" Sam asked.

"It always was. I guess it'll be worth double to triple now.

"What happened? How was she, er, killed? Who did it?"

"We're investigating that, now," I answered. "You have

to be informed that you're a suspect, but I guess you know that."

"*Me?!*" he squealed. "But ... why would I kill her? This is insane! You're crazy!"

"You stand to make a bundle on her art, now that she's dead, now don't you?" Sam asked.

"*Me*?! You're crazy! I work for the art gallery! I won't make anything at all from it! You're crazy! My god! You're both crazy! I'm having a nightmare! You're crazy!"

"I didn't ever think you had anything to do with it," I said. "It didn't make any sense. Maybe if you were one of the owners or if you have a contract with her that would put you in the middle of it. It should be easy enough to prove you didn't do it. Where were you at three in the morning of the first?"

"In the hotel, asleep! My god! I don't even know where she lives! I only know I'm to come here to this house and crate the stuff she's marked for sale and accompany it back to New York!

"My god!"

"I don't suppose you had company?" I asked.

"Of course not! My god! Wait a minute! Wait one minute! It takes almost an hour to drive out here from the hotel! I was in the bar until it closed at three o'clock! They stayed open an extra hour because it was New Years Eve! They had a kind of special permit! I sat at the bar and talked to the barmaid while she cleaned up. She'll be able to vouch for me. Her name was Susanne. She was asking about New York because she's taking a course in modeling and wants to go there. I told her these local agencies tend to teach them to keep a big ridiculous smile on their face when they talk and it's a big laugh to the better agencies because it only looks silly and false, so she'll be able to remember me."

"She wasn't killed in this area, but you couldn't have gotten from the airport to her place in the time. That outs you out of it, if your girlfriend will vouch for you."

"You can't take any of this stuff yet," Sam said. "I don't know if you can take any of it, anytime, unless you have some kind of agreement or something."

He said there was a signed exclusive sales agreement with the galleries, so it shouldn't be hard to straighten that part of it out. We left him crating the stuff and looked the place over very carefully. I found a little box of photographs. They were very interesting. They were nude studies of several of the people who were at my party. There were code numbers on the back of each one. They were all males.

There were racks of paintings along one wall, each one with a code number on the frame under the slot. I found one that matched a photograph and slid the painting out.

Steve Keene, in a pose a little bit different than the photo, looked out at me through sleepy eyes. She had slightly enhanced the musculature and had taken the slight paunch away a bit and had changed the features a little to accent his better qualities. The pose was artistic and somewhat erotic, but it was definitely not pornographic, in any way.

"Jeez! That's that Keene guy!" Sam said. "She was *good!*"

"Miss Bond was a truly superb artist," Henley lectured. "She has produced some of the finest nude studies we've ever seen, though her main theme in many of the paintings was fantasy landscapes and mythological studies. She also produced some fine statues – she sculpted as well as she painted – of nudes that are, in my very humble opinion, unsurpassed."

I started sliding out various works at random and noted a number of faces I was familiar with, to one extent or another.

Norm Schultz and Bill Kocsis, I recognized.

I was stopped cold by one of them.

"Somebody you know?" Sam asked.

"My god! If he really looks like that I'd go queer for him!" Hensley cried, then blushed. "It's a joke that we're all supposed to be queer who work in the galleries. I'm *not*, but even Burt Reynolds once said something like that on national TV! That is one beautiful man, and he's as sexy as anything I've ever seen, male *or* female!"

"The strange thing is, he looks *just* like that, except for the sexy pose. She didn't enhance anything."

"Who is it?" Sam asked.

"His name's Mike Nelson. He runs the private airport where I keep my jet. He's always seemed such a true innocent to me. He even blushes sometimes – a lot, really. I just can't picture him and Bonnie."

I went through the photos until I found the one with the code for that painting. It was Mike in his regular cutoff jeans and nothing else on the beach. She had undressed him and given him the sexy expression, but the painting was him exactly and looked so lifelike I could almost expect him to grin and blush because anyone saw him in the pose.

He was in a classic pose, semi-reclining on a large weathered driftwood stump, but the sexy expression was an open invitation. It looked perfectly natural with the beach behind. Mike belongs in that kind of setting.

"He *is* just like that!" Hensley said. "I don't ever want to meet him! Not after I said that!"

"Afraid he'd rape you?" Sam asked.

"I'm afraid he wouldn't *have* to! If I ever met him I'd picture that painting and that look."

I said I wished there was some way I could buy that painting without breaking any laws. Hensley said none of the paintings still in the racks were part of the show – though they probably *all* would be now. "I'll call Yagob and ask him if he'll take an offer on one of the nudes and explain it's a friend of a friend and he'll probably let me take a bid on it, but I have to tell you he won't entertain a bid of less than eight thousand for one of Bonnie's nude studies. He's never taken less than that for a nude by her."

"It's good quality art. Tell him I'll offer twelve five, which I think is a fair price, all around." We agreed that I could buy it and anything else I wanted to bid on after the stuff was released.

We'd have to match the work with photos and with suspects. There were several comic semi-nudes. One was of an old man looking lost and in pain as he looked at a nude woman's leg and thigh sticking out from under the covers on a bed and a woman's hand with the finger giving the "Come here" crook. It was obvious the fellow was impotent without it being shown directly.

Another was a preacher in a black robe behind a lectern. The robe was caught on the corner of the podium and the cut off pant legs were tied to his calves with hairy bare legs showing up past the calves. It was the standard portrayal of a flasher, just with the cleric's robe instead of the trench coat. The preacher was holding up a Bible in one hand and a tight clenched fist with the other. She had captured the studied pious look beautifully. I was amazed at how she used a comic pose – and came up with what I would say is definitely art!

I wondered if there had been something on that order with Karl Forbes as subject. If so, he would have been after the photo or the painting, or both. It was far too possible any of the men in the photos wanted the pictures back, but maybe not. I made up my mind to ask Mike about it and see what he had to say.

We secured the house and left a guard on it. There would never be one minute that house wasn't under close surveillance. If our murderer found out about it and had wanted one of those photos or paintings he wasn't going to get it. It really wasn't legal, but Sam let me take both the painting and photograph of Mike. I signed a use agreement with the police department and am a certified state crime investigator, making it all technically legal.

I went home, showed the painting and photo to Alma, who said she wanted that painting to hang in the Florida room. I told her I'd already put in a bid on it.

I took the photo and painting, put them in the little Cessna, and flew down to the private airport to show the painting to Mike. He looked at it with a critical eye, and said, "It's kinda good, isn't it?

"Bonnie said the paintings were all sold in New York, so no one would ever know about them here, but I didn't care. She sure makes me look sexy, doesn't she?"

"You know she's dead?"

"Dead?! No! She's neurotic as hell, and she's a nympho, but a lot of artists are like that. I didn't hear anything about her dying!"

"She was murdered. Her real name was Bonnie Patrick.

She was at a party at my place early on New Years Eve and was found murdered the next morning. It was in the papers down there."

"I read about a murder in a pool house or something down there and thought you'd be in on it, but I didn't connect the name. I'm sorry to hear it, but she would come on to any guy, so I guess somebody's wife got her. She took some silly chances."

"You don't care about the painting? You don't care she did a nude of you?"

He shrugged. "Why not? There's isn't anything wrong with it. I think it's good."

"It *is* good. I'm buying it. Alma wants to put it in the Florida room in Bonita."

He blushed, grinned, and said, "I didn't stop to think maybe somebody like Alma would ever see it. I don't really mind, but you know.... It's Alma, who I know."

"Alma likes to look as much as I do, we just stop before we do more than look. You knew Bonnie was going to do a nude painting of you?"

"Yeah. She had this little album of lots of pictures of her paintings that showed what she did, like how she changed the features to take out little imperfections and changed an angle or a curve to make it look more what she called `classical.' She said she wouldn't have to change me much, because I'm a natural.

"It's funny, in an odd sort of way. She didn't have anything she wouldn't do and she liked raunchy videos and those party films, but she would never paint anything like that, herself. Her stuff is really good."

"It is. Do you know if she told all of the guys she was going to do the nude paintings of them?"

. "Well, she told me. She had the little book and a few pictures like that and showed how she would maybe make some guy's stomach flatter and put some muscle here and there and take fat away. You can see how she changed little things like the nose and eyebrows. She said she looked for the basic bone structure and that kind of thing. She could paint what a guy *should* look like if men would have the willpower to take care of themselves.

"She said I could see the painting after it was finished, if I liked, but I know she didn't let most guys."

"I take it you slept with her?"

"Well. we went to bed a couple of times, but we didn't sleep." He blushed. "She claimed it would give her the correct perspective about how to represent a guy on canvas to first get to know him on linen."

We talked awhile, then I went back to Bonita Springs and took the painting and photo to the house. I'd been thinking about what Mike said, so went to the police station to see Sam.

"Mike said Bonnie carried a little book with photos of the paintings and the pictures she worked from to explain what she would do to the models," I reported. "He said there were quite a few pictures of guys, but he didn't know but a couple of them. He said he saw someone now and then who he could recognize from the photos.

"I didn't see any such book at the house out there or here. I think that book is what she was killed for. I think that's what the search was all about."

"Then we have to find it if she hid it someplace around her place," Sam replied. "If someone else has it now, it'll be the killer. He may have found it and destroyed it."

"No. I have a very strong feeling he wouldn't destroy it. You have all those photos here from the house, don't you?"

He agreed they were in the evidence room, so we used the lab to make copies of all of them. I took each picture as it came out to try to identify the subject. There were forty four of them from that file and a lot more in another box the crew found. The ones we had were the most recent.

There were paintings and codes for seventeen of them. Some had no code and probably weren't going to end up as paintings, some had codes, but no paintings. We assumed they were planned for use.

"What do you have?" Sam asked.

"Steve Keene, photo and painting. Jim Tooney, photo and painting. Two photos. Paul Allen, photo, but no painting. Bill Kocsis, both photo and painting. Norm Schultz, photo and painting. Tom Billings, photo, but no painting – and that one interests me quite a lot – Dave Weitz, photo, but no painting.

"I want to look at all the photos from the older box. I might be able to learn a lot."

"They're right here. Why the big interest in Billings?"

"He's from Maryland. He hasn't been here very long."

"The photo was taken the same place a lot of them were – in her bedroom. I meant to tell you. Hensley called to say you could buy the painting of your friend for twelve five.

"What do you see, so far?"

"I have to see that book! We have to find it! There's no doubt it was copies of these photos here, and maybe some older ones she'd done paintings of. Our answer's bound to be in that book. It has to be. Her killer was looking for that book because it has something deadly in it."

"She wasn't doing the blackmail bit with the stuff, as you

learned. Maybe the guy who has the book now plans to do a little profitable dealing with it? Maybe the *killer* wants to try the blackmail angle?"

"It's far too possible, for my tastes. I think we could thwart any such scheme by letting every single one of the subjects know we have the originals. My fear is that there might be someone shown in that book who's not in this collection. It's far too possible the killer didn't find that book. She didn't have it on her and he searched the trailer amateurishly.

"We have to try to find it, if only to have the smug feeling the killer didn't get what he killed her for."

"OK. Let's look at it from this angle: Did your friend in the painting come here to see the book or did she have it with her on the beach – or wherever?"

"She went to Sarasota with a man who kept a plane at the field Mike owns. She met him there and they stayed the night at the house on Englewood Beach the kid gave him. She took the picture the next morning when he was out on the beach. She showed him the photos, then, and again on another trip. Apparently, she thought he was worth several trips.

"He said the book is one of those leather photo albums you can buy at any discount store. Brown, about ten by twelve. It had six photos of people with the photo of the painting beside it per double page and was full, except for the last page and a half. There were probably eighteen to twenty pages."

"Roughly fifty subjects. Go through these pictures and pick out any you want copied."

I spent about an hour selecting nine more pictures from the older group. Jim Tooney, Norm Schultz, Steve Keene and Bill Kocsis were repeats. The others were faces that seemed familiar. I had the copies to try to identify them. None were from my party group. Some of the photos had codes on them, some didn't.

I crosschecked and found the codes were a bit different than on the paintings in the newer box, so suggested there were a few who had more than one painting of themselves. The older ones were already sold.

There were two other codes for Tooney, one for Schultz, one for Bill Kocsis and two for Steve Keene.

"Well. I'll spend tomorrow discreetly showing these the photos and asking about them without telling anyone of any pictures of others. I mainly want to see the reactions of the various people to learning that we have the pictures. It usually doesn't work, but, every now and then, someone gives something away with a reaction. I still think our killer is one of the eight."

"Eight? Oh, yeah. Hensley has an alibi. It checked out. He was at the bar until three o'clock. He didn't have any motive I can see, anyhow. He just works for the art gallery."

"Just so he doesn't get a huge bonus when this stuff's sold. He didn't have time to do it, so his boss didn't hire him to kill her.

"I'll check whatever I can of this stuff out tomorrow and let you know if I learn anything new. I have a nagging feeling about something, but it'll have to come in its own time. It's vague. I've seen or heard something, maybe it was at the party, maybe later. It's connected with the pool – or the towel – or the state of her clothes. I think."

We said our goodbyes and I went home to a delicious dinner. I later showed Alma the photos. She said she was sorry there wasn't one of Sean McMullins with a twinkle in her eye. "He and Lorna came over this afternoon in their mullet boat, and we chatted. Lorna got me aside and told me about her conversation with you.

"Sean is *some hunk*, you know!"

"So am I, if you can believe Lorna. She's a hell of a lot of woman!"

"Oh, I know you're a hunk, but I've had *you* already! I wonder?"

"Maybe we could swap mates or something."

We ended up all over the big sofa doing depraved things to one another – things that are none of your business!

In the morning I called on Steve Keene outside of his trailer and showed him his picture. He said he knew Bonnie was planning to paint him as a nude study, but she said the painting would go to New York and no one would know. There had been a couple, he thought. It was much the same as she had told Mike, except she changed a lot on his painting. She had taken several years from his age, gotten rid of the pot, thickened and darkened the hair, and changed the eyes, very slightly. Steve asked if it was going to be necessary to show the picture around.

"I doubt it. She had pictures of several other people. I want all of you to know we have them in case someone has the idea of a little blackmail – or anything."

I hinted we believed there was a set of pictures missing – and someone might want to sell people their pictures to avoid having them given to the wife. We would want to know who and everything about the attempt, should that happen. He promised he'd let us know and thanked me for not letting Helen know about it.

Norm Schultz was mowing around the pool at the clubhouse, meaning it was easy to show him the pictures. He turned red and stuttered a bit and said his marriage would be ruined if Pat found out. I reassured him the pictures wouldn't be shown to anyone but the subjects. I warned him about the blackmail possibility and he said there was no way he'd pay any scumball blackmail. We could very damned well count on him to tell us if anyone approached him with anything – if he didn't break their goddamned neck first.

I caught Jim Tooney at work and took him aside. He said he couldn't care less about the pictures and we could print them in the newspapers, if we liked. He'd knock anybody on their ass who tried to blackmail him.

Dave Weitz went into his private office with me and sweated and moaned. I told him the pictures weren't going to be shown to anyone else, but there may be a blackmail attempt. He must let us know, fast, if that happened. He stammered a bit more and halfheartedly agreed to cooperate if we could just guarantee to keep it from Sylvia.

Bill Kocsis was at the country club, playing an early round of golf. I went out and walked along with him. He was a little worried about the pictures, but stated he'd weathered the storm already. It wouldn't be so bad. He'd let us know if anyone tried any blackmail.

Tom Billings was almost incoherent with rage. He insisted she swore no one would ever see any of it, either in Florida or in Maryland, and he'd blow the head off of anyone who had the abject stupidity to try to blackmail *him*! I thought the reaction was far too much. It seemed more like an act than real rage.

Paul Allen was almost in tears about it. He kept saying he

must have been out of his mind to allow Bonnie to take those pictures! He said he'd let us know if anyone so much as mentioned the pictures to him.

The next stop was the police station, then Sam Lukens, Dan Ford, and I went back to Bonnie's trailer and looked everywhere. It wasn't in the trailer itself, so we checked the tool shed and the porches and carport, then Dan went through the car carefully. He had a lot of experience looking for drugs. He knew the clever hiding places. It wasn't there.

"Either the killer found it or she had it very well hidden," Sam said, after about three hours of searching. "I don't know where else to look! There isn't an inch we missed here!"

"I can think of one place," Dan suggested. "It's another trick some drug dealers use. It's the old purloined letter trick.

"Where would a book go unnoticed?"

We went back inside to look over the books in the trailer. There was a full set of encyclopedias, several Harlequin romance novels, a few Forbes magazines, some cook-books, a big stack of old Wall Street Journals and some old New York newspapers with blurbs about her shows or with stories about art and jewel thefts.

"If it's here I'd say hidden in an encyclopedia," Dan said. "Nothing else is big enough to cover it."

We took each volume out and opened it. The "Plaza – Quest" volume had the pages glued together and the center cut out so the album fit snugly into it. Sam said he had it as soon as he pulled the book. It was quite a bit lighter than any of the other volumes.

But there simply weren't any photos there that weren't

copies of ones we already had. We saw pictures of several paintings that weren't in the collection and figured they'd probably been sold – but there weren't any pictures we didn't already have. Period.

"Either there's something in one or more of these pictures we've been overlooking or he killed her thinking this was the only set of pictures," Sam said. "The only other thing I can think of is that this wasn't what the killer was searching for."

"This has to be it," I argued. "There's something we don't know or she was killed, as you said, because the killer didn't think there was another set of the pictures. We have the entire answer in our hands, right now, but it's still in some foreign language.

"Cripes! I even sound corny to myself!

"I do tend to wonder if maybe there was something in one of the pictures that would incriminate her killer for something more than a little dalliance with her. Maybe...."

"What do you mean?" Sam asked.

"Maybe one of the photos showed something other than just the guy in a sexy pose. We'll have to study all those backgrounds of the photos with a magnifying lens."

"Most of the photos seem to have been taken in her own bedroom, twenty feet from here," Sam replied. "It should be easy to take the ones taken somewhere else out of the stack and enlarge them."

"It could be one taken in her bedroom. It could be something on the night table or something."

"Whatever, it will mean a lot of work," he said with a heavy sigh. "That's part of the job. We might as well get on with it."

Chapter four

I leaned back and thought for a few minutes to get my ideas straight. It was entirely possible there was nothing on those photos and it was the paintings themselves the killer wanted to keep from being seen by a wife or something. On the other hand, she was killed and the search was made at what had to be a great risk to the killer.

The killer knew about the album. She showed it to him or told him something about something in the album at my party, and he killed her before the next day dawned. That might mean she was very close to taking some kind of action concerning whatever it was.

Was the killing premeditated to the extent the killer knew he was going to have to act *before* the party? Was I concentrating on the party too much?

If it was something planned earlier, Bonnie's killer must have approached her at the party to try to talk her out of doing whatever it was. I had to concentrate on my party and the people there from a single angle, and only that angle, then it wouldn't matter – there wasn't any reason for her to have gone to a gathering of people who she knew either despised her or would be forced to avoid her. Only Jim Tooney could very well have much to do with her there. It then became apparent she didn't leave the party because of Alma's ploy, but because she took care of what she came there for in the first place.

What was that?

She set up an assignation appointment at the pool with her killer, then went somewhere else to a party, then returned home, got her bathing suit, hid the album, and went to her death.

I would have to find where she went, in the meanwhile. I had to account for her actions from when she left my party until she arrived at the pool. Maybe, then, I would know why.

There was that nagging again. What had I seen or heard? What made me stop to think every time I passed the point of her going to that pool?

OK. It was obvious it was someone close who wouldn't be missed elsewhere while he/she went to the pool, but that was everybody who lived in the trailer court. Did that mean I could eliminate looking anywhere else? Hadn't I, already?

It would come in its own time. I knew better than to try to rush what my subconscious saw.

It was unlikely blackmail was involved here. She had more money than she knew what to do with, already. She was sexually oriented, not monetarily.

I had to go through the photos in the album. They were the ones that counted. It's possible she was blackmailing someone in some form for something other than money.

Sam came in with another box of photos. I groaned, but he said they weren't pictures of people, they were pictures of things. I glanced through them, then went back through more slowly. Sam asked me what I'd seen.

"It may not be important, but it could be. This is a picture of a driftwood stump. Look at it."

He studied it for a minute, then said, "It's the wood your friend, Mike, was posed on. It's the entire background, including the pelican and gulls. Even the shells laying all around it are the same. There's that piece of seaweed on that urchin and the mangrove seeds exactly the way ...

exactly the same!

"That's why it looked so natural. She painted the scene and put your friend in it. Nothing contrived, really."

"These are all pictures of backgrounds for the paintings, I think. That means there may be a picture of whatever the killer wanted, right here, separate from the person shown with whatever it is. I think we have a whole lot more to look for than some small detail in a photo in that album, but I *do* have an idea or two!"

"Lead on, MacBeth! I don't know where you're going with this, but I see your point. The paintings may be far more important than the photos."

"We have to look at all the paintings, match the background photo to the work, and also put the model photo with it. We may find what we're after, that way. It could take all three things to make the motive."

I opened the album to the first picture. It was of someone not included in our investigation. There was no one on the first two pages we were concerned with but Jim Tooney in an old pose. He had been about five years younger and in much better physical shape, for that painting. He was shown semi-reclining on the bed in her bedroom in the photo. There was a code in marker ink on the bottom left margin of the photo, so I searched through the backgrounds for the same code. There were two photos of him from different angles with one of the background scene. It was a beach scene with sea oats, sand, shells and small bits of detritus. The painting was of him standing with the sun to the far side and ahead of him, slightly, making a fuzziness to his upper outline very much like what you see when you look too directly toward the sun. He was standing back about three feet from where the waves washed in looking at his feet with a slight smile on his face. He was picking up a large redhorse conch shell with a toe and was reaching for it with one hand, as if he'd that instant started the motion. It looked very real.

He was nude in the painting, as in the photo, but the position of the body and the slightly lifted leg in the painting hid the genitalia. It was impressive, innocent – and definitely art. She had enhanced the definition of his outline with a brightness that gave the picture a feeling both of fantasy and reality at the same time.

"Pretty good, isn't it? I sort of get the idea. It's what should be, but isn't."

"Partly that, and partly her feelings about him. It's the way the world *is*. The beach exists and the man exists, but it's a thing that can't be at the same time. The reality is that the world won't allow this at the time and place. It's an ideal that could be, but isn't. She took the reality and inserted a dream into it, thus the position of the light and the slight fuzziness of his outline.

"*Damn*, she was *good*!"

"She has to be good if I can understand it from looking at a picture of the painting.".

I grinned, and went on. The next picture I came to involving any of our group was of Steve Keene. He was shown sitting on a white marble bench reading a book, Agatha Christie's *And Then There Were None*. There was a bottle of Harvey's Bristol Cream and a glass to one side. He had a pipe in one hand and the book in the other. It was as good a painting as the one of Tooney. The plantings looked alive, but this one was solid reality.

Sam looked through the background photos and found the picture of the garden and the picture of a counter with that book and a bottle of Harvey's and a glass on it. There was the pipe in an ashtray on the counter by the wine.

"One thing looks pretty sure. She painted in every least little detail from models. Everything. It's all exact. That's why it looks so natural. See the water stain on the book in the background picture? It's in the painting! Right there! See the water ring? It looks like someone put a wet glass on the book, at some time. It's a detail that makes the scene look real. She was *good*! You don't have to explain much about this one!"

The next was of Norman Schultz. There was a detailed background photo of a den/library with a desk, the green-shaded lamp, the pen desk set – everything was natural looking. The brown leather chairs looked downright inviting. There was a stack of papers on the corner of the desk and a few stock certificates spread across the inkmat. There was an open case of jewelry. There were silver trophies in a case. There were pictures of a family.

This painting was highly shadowed and somewhat dark. He was in a smoking jacket that was hanging open, holding up a pendant with a large emerald surrounded by brilliant diamonds. The scene was rich. That's the only thing to call it. Wealth oozed from the work, but it was a cold ostentatious type of wealth. It didn't attract, rather, it repulsed.

"She saw him like that?" Sam asked, then shrugged and shook his head.

"She saw a grasping greedy side to him. I didn't detect that in him, at all, but I'll defer to her. She was expert at seeing through people, it seems. I don't think that one missed much when it came to her artist persona."

The next was of Bill Kocsis. He was shown doing a swan

dive into a blue brick-lined pool from some rocks with bromeliads and ferns growing on them. It was a view one would see if he were watching the dive from across the pool – mostly the back, but the head was back enough and the angle was upward enough that the viewer was looking straight into his eyes. It was good, but not of the quality of the first three. She had written "Ugh!" under it, so she felt she had failed to capture exactly what she wanted. She was honest enough to include it in the album, I guess to show she wasn't always perfect and couldn't guarantee every picture would be a masterpiece.

There were two poses of him, one in her bedroom and the other on a beach, somewhere. There was a background photo of a rocky waterfall in a landscape arrangement somewhere, one of a pool with red brick lining and one of the tropical plants. Bromeliads and ferns.

"She put the broken brick in right there and the dead leaves on that pineapple thing and that gunky slime on those rocks," Sam said. "It looks real, but I see she didn't like it much. I don't know enough about it to know if this is as good as the one of your friend. I guess even she missed what she wanted, sometimes."

"The one of Tooney is good and the one of Keene is. The one of Norm Schultz isn't quite up to her standard. This isn't good, at all, to her standards, though it's a hell of a lot better than most.

"She didn't capture anything about Kocsis. It's just some naked guy diving into a swimming pool. His expression is both arrogant and a little cruel, which is all she could find to say about him.

"Maybe she found there just wasn't anything about him to show. He seemed a bit shallow to me when I met him.

Yuppie type.

"Her paintings tell you a lot about the model. This really could be the best of the lot – because she defined a person with few or no redeeming features. He was there, but the background would be better off without him. He's like a pretty but cheap trinket. He disturbs the reality around him by wandering through life, never really seeing, hearing, tasting, smelling or feeling anything. He's there, but so what?

"My god! She *didn't* miss what she wanted to express! I think maybe the `Ugh!' is about him, not the painting.

"That's the thing about real art. You don't necessarily see the point at first glance. You have to think about it.

"This is good. This is very good – and this tells us a lot about her *and* about him. Little Bonnie was a very deep person. She tells us a lot in her paintings. She could probably only communicate completely in the art, and didn't have any real conception of how to say a thing with words. She took all these guys to bed because she didn't know what else to do. The one of Tooney tells you this is a man who is not afraid of life, who looks to the future, and who fits in with nature, which is what she saw in him at the time.

"The one of Keene shows a studious man – something she saw in him that I missed, but the way she captured that tells me he's exactly that kind when he's alone. Keene will be a reader and a quiet type who's really very deep. She said so much more than a book could hope.... The one of Schultz shows she thought he was the type who thinks he was born to be very rich. There's just enough greed in his expression to tell the viewer he hadn't really made it. This painting would make a good classroom example of how to use subliminals in art. The whole story is there in a much more detailed way than you could write in any book!

"See the way his hand is a fist holding the necklace? That's the desire to possess. The other hand is limp, like he doesn't quite know what to do with it, now that he has it. Defeatism. Try, but you'll miss!

"There's all that quietly beautiful stuff on the desk, but he's after the flashiest piece there. The stocks represent the true wealth he's passed over to get the flash. The jewel chest is on top of the stocks. Note how he's just before biting his lower lip.

"He wants security. He knows he's already missed the important part. He's confused and frustrated. He can't understand why everything he touches ends up hollow. He has no idea what he really wants.

"This is more than good. It's genius!

"Note the picture of the wife and the pictures of the kids are behind the stacks of papers and how the jewel chest has pushed the picture of the wife aside. Wife and family are the second or third priority to him.

"Bonnie Bond was a true genius! Bonnie Patrick was a nympho, and neurotic as hell. What Bonnie had to say was said through the art. She wasn't fooled by people, very often, I'll wager! She saw right through to what a person is and she painted it as it is!

"Remember the painting I'm buying? Think of it and tell me something about Mike Nelson."

He screwed up his face, then said, "He's sexy as hell, and innocent about it. He's the type everybody likes. He'll give you his last thin dime, and he's loyal. If you cross him, he'll never trust you again, no matter what. He's something of a hedonist by nature, but there's some kind of conflict inside. He's always a bit unsure of ... of whether ... a thing's *right*! A sort of moral thing. What he's been taught in church or in school doesn't really match up with the real world.

"I think she just said, `This is the most natural person I ever met. No frills and no gimmicks. What you see is what you get – and you get plenty.'

"I mean, that's from the woman's perspective, but the guy is sexy as hell and he doesn't mean to be.

"Close?"

"That's Mike. He's completely natural and he's sexy as hell without trying to be or even knowing he is. Bonnie was a genius because she used the little details you don't even know you're seeing to tell you things. You could hold an advanced class in art appreciation with any of her paintings. You could hold a whole course! It's all here, but it has to come from inside the artist. That's what makes it art.

"There's a later painting of Keene and a later one of Tooney in this album. I want to see how and how much they changed, to her way of thinking."

I found the one of Tooney near the back of the album. He was laying on his left side on a leather couch, full frontal nudity with a slight leer on his face. There was a table in front of the couch with a tall can of beer sitting on it, a Field and Stream magazine toward one side and a Penthouse on the other. There was a TV remote control device on top of the Penthouse with a TV Guide next to it and a few CD boxes of Dolly Parton and the Judds. The place looked a little dingy. There wasn't much to it. The background photo was of the exact scene without Tooney in it.

"That's his living room!" Sam exclaimed. "I questioned him in there! He sat on that couch!"

"Uh-huh. Can you see what she saw in him by this time?"

"He's a redneck male chauvinist pig! She must have had a spat with him when she did that one. That's a nowhere guy who thinks he's god's own gift to women.

"She really *was* a genius if I can see those kinds of thing in her work. You don't think she could actually corrupt me enough that I'd like this art stuff, do you?"

"She damned well had the power. She also made him attractive, in his own way, so she said he was a redneck male chauvinist pig that she couldn't stay away from because he was sexy to her."

The next one of Steve Keene showed him sitting on an old dock ,dangling his feet in the water at sunset. The sunset was past and in front of him and was one of those rose, red and gold ones we have so often here that fade to dark purple just before it gets dark. He had a rod and reel leaning against a post of the dock, a bait bucket next to him, and a faraway look on his face as he stared at the sunset hues ahead. There was a book about sailboats laying open behind him.

"She hadn't changed her mind about him one bit," Sam suggested, simply.

I nodded. "That one is pure art. That one would bring a fortune."

"She took a little weight off his middle and softened the line of his jaw, just a bit. He's lumpier than that. She sort of smoothed out the rough edges, didn't she?"

"She didn't *see* any rough edges on him. She obviously was in love with him. That doesn't mean anything, really. She may have fallen in love with a lot of her models, simply so she could paint them as perfection."

"Pure method acting?" he asked, and I nodded again. I was surprising myself by finding a great and growing respect for Bonnie Bond. I found myself wondering how she would have painted me. I wondered how she could paint all these innocent scenes that almost no one could call pornographic – I thought of the Forbes prudes, and grinned – yet they were erotic as hell. They were erotic *because* they weren't cheap pornography.

I went back to the album, but that seemed to be all it had to offer.

"Well, I think now we can pretty much concentrate our attention on Keene, Schultz, Kocsis and Tooney. They would be the ones who want this album – logically. It may be that someone else *thought* he was in it, so we can't eliminate anyone else she had any pictures of."

"Someone else may have seen the album and she might have been mad enough because they grabbed at it or something to have told them they should see their own portrayal. I think you have one special little problem in it the way you're going at it."

"What's that?"

"You said she must have shown something in it to someone at the party, but all the women were watching her, so how could she manage that one? Also, did you ever see the album in her hands – or anywhere else? She damned well wasn't carrying it around with her!"

"She drifted around before she left. She went to her car and almost no one noticed until they heard the motor start. Someone could have gone to her car with her to look at the album without being seen."

He agreed anything was possible.

He was having a background check done on the Billings, in Maryland. I decided to see some of the people still on the list to try to eliminate a few more. I also wanted to find where she went after my party, so I asked Sam.

"We're not sure yet, but Dan Ford suggested she used to go to several of the clubs at times. A couple of them were having New Years parties. He's checking them out. If she left another party with someone, we're doing all this stuff for nothing – no, I guess not. It was someone who would find that pool convenient, which eliminates a casual pickup at a bar."

"I'll call later to see what you know. You have my list and what I've found. I put my reasons for my own conclusions in."

"We'll stay in touch. I'll have blowups made of all the stuff we sat aside here and get you copies. Maybe you can teach me something about art from them – but I could do with nude women instead of nude men."

I laughed and went out to my Jeep to sit for a minute, then started it and headed for Selma's place. She wasn't in, so I went back to the pool area and through. There were several people sitting around in the lounge chairs, but all on the opposite side from where Selma found Bonnie. Selma came over from the office to greet me, and we talked. I got her impressions of my major suspects.

"Jim Tooney? Sort of what we all called `redneck pig' when I was young. Guzzles cheap beer, watches football and basketball on TV, believes strongly in a double standard, and thinks he's god's gift to women."

"Redneck male chauvinist pig?"

She grinned and nodded, then asked why I chose that particular description.

"We were looking at a picture of a painting Bonnie did of him, recently. Sam Lukens said she made him look like a redneck male chauvinist pig. She was one hell of a fine artist, regardless of what else she was.

"Steve Keene?"

"A fantastic and very real jewel! He's really a quiet type who's a lot deeper than that friendly bear. He's really very shy, or solitary, at least. Next to Sean McMullin, he's the truly sexiest person in the state. It's a quiet sexuality.

"What did la whore say about him in her painting?"

"That he was a studious, solitary man by nature and was very deep – and she was completely in love with him when she painted the picture," I said, watching for her reaction.

"I imagine she could convince herself she was in love with anyone. Did she really capture that much of him? Of all of them?"

"Yes. I'll show you some of the stuff as soon as I can. You can see one of her paintings at my place. It's of a friend of ours from Englewood. Alma hung it in the Florida room. I think you'll agree *he's* the sexiest man in the US of A when you see that picture. She painted him exactly as he is."

"Your wife will show me a picture of the sexiest man in the world she's hanging in your Florida room? A nude?" she asked with a leer.

"I bought it! You'll have to meet Mike. He's a total innocent, in some ways, which makes him that much sexier to women.

"Norm Schultz?"

"Another true jewel. He's maybe a little too ambitious, but he's a doll. He really dotes on Pat. She's his whole life, really.

"Just what Bonnie painted?"

"Not even close. Bill Kocsis?"

"A standard yuppie type, but he's all right. He wants things, but he has values. He's a little deeper than people tend to think, but maybe not a whole lot. He has his place. I suppose she saw him as something very special?"

"You hit two dead on the head and were way off with two. She viewed him as not having any redeeming qualities, whatever. She saw him as something pretty to have around, but not a thing of any value. He's just happens to be ... there."

"Oh? I suppose Tom Billings would be next on your list. I don't know much about him, but he's the type who's just like everybody else. She'd make him a Norman Rockwell standard type. I don't think she'd make him sexy, so I don't see him as a nude study – though maybe she saw something I didn't.

"She wouldn't paint Bat, because he'd cause her trouble. They got along because Bat and Kitty are old enough and sure enough of themselves to not allow something like Bonnie to screw up their lives.

"She wouldn't paint Sean nude – because he'd say it wasn't right. Even *she* wouldn't do anything he asked her not to.

"Dave Weitz. I can't see it. He's not the nude model type at all. She'd put him in a toga or something and make him a very rich man with concubines all around, giving him sneers behind his back.

"Paul Allen would be shown in a suburban setting taking a sunbath by a pool. He's the suburban type.

"Any more questions?"

"Just one more. How do you know about all the nude

paintings? I thought you didn't know about her art, except for the statues."

"Uh-oh! You've got me! I'll confess! I knew I'd have to slip up somewhere, sooner or later!" She cried, causing the people to stare at us. "It's actually quite simple. Connie told me about her nudes and showed me a catalog of one show she had in New York. Jim Tooney wasn't shown as a pig in that one! He was on a beach with a conch shell on his toe. It was a truly magnificent piece!

"There were four other nudes in the show, but only Jim was anyone I recognized. I have to admit she was good. Very good."

"I think there were two of her. I think Bonnie Patrick was a nympho bitch. I think Bonnie Bond was a true genius and as superb an artist as I've ever seen. Photographs of her work don't show half of it. You have to directly view some of the paintings."

"You could invite me to lunch at your place and show me the friend your wife likes so much she hangs a nude painting of in your Florida room," she suggested with a grin – so I said, "Why not come with me to my place to see an etching or two? We could grab a snack!"

She went inside to tell Mrs. Bellows she was leaving for an hour or so, then we drove to my place. Alma fixed us some crab salad and grilled cheese sandwiches, then took Selma into the Florida room to show her the painting of Mike. I heard Selma tell Alma I had really told the truth when I said he was the sexiest man in the world – if he really looked even slightly like that.

"He looks exactly like that!" Alma replied. "There are some photos in the desk. He's bound to be in some of them. He doesn't get that sexy look on his face. He doesn't realize he's so sexy. He actually *blushes* all the time! Talk about *sexy*! He's a total innocent! He really is! Here. That was at Englewood. We'd been out fishing and he was wrestling around with CD and Jim. That's why he's all wet. They throw each other in the canal.

"That's Cal Jones and his wife, Wilma. He's FHP ... and Wilma and Lou, she's not in this one ... here she is. That's Paulo, her husband, and those are our kids. Cedric David, Scott McDade, and our daughter, Bonnie Alma.

"I almost want to change her name from Bonnie, after meeting that woman. She was so vindictive, but she really only needed someone to care about her. She didn't know the first thing about communication on a personal level – with other women.

"That's Cal and Wilma's daughter, Allie, and that's Lou and Paulo's son, Paul."

"To hell with all that!" Selma cried. "Who is this Jim? My god! This one looks like he should be a dozen Bonnie Bond paintings! He's totally, absolutely beautiful!"

They giggled a lot and chatted about our friends while I went out to the orchid houses to check on the watering and humidity. There was a Blc cross blooming for the first time that was really spectacular in its own way. It was a multiple parentage cross that had come through with every art shade imaginable. The form and texture were good, but the colors were amazing. There were about twenty in bloom at the time, but there had been only buds a week before.

Alma brought Selma in behind me. I heard her gasp.

"That one's a lot like Blc. My-My," Alma noted. "I'm glad you used that good dark one as a parent."

"We have everything from white with colored lip to very

dark, and from light pink to bright yellow. There are a lot of art shades. I have no idea where the green one comes from."

"Brassavola digbyana and Blc. Ojai are in the parentage, so a couple are likely," Alma pointed out. "I heard the `art shades' bit, so you've decided to name it after her?"

"I'll name it Blc. Memoria Bonnie Bond, in honor of the artist personality. I think she was schizophrenic, in a strange way. I don't consider Bonnie Patrick and Bonnie Bond to be the same person, really."

"Oh, Alma! I've never seen a blue orchid before!" Selma cried, looking at the several divisions of Sheila's Sapphire in bloom.

"That was CD's grandmother's most famous blue cross," Alma said. "It's been used as a parent a lot. It breeds true, which is *very* rare with blues – and blues are rare, in themselves. That one can be hard to grow, but this Blue Forever is easy. You can just hang it under a tree and take it in if we're predicted to have a freeze."

Alma handed her a plant with four buds on one stem and three on another. They would open in a few days. She gasped again and tried to refuse to take it, but no one refuses Alma. She said we have six or seven pieces of that plant. We don't need more.

We went back inside, chatted a few more minutes, and I drove her back to the community center. There wasn't much happening there and I didn't see anything I'd missed earlier, so I left and headed for the Kocsis place.

I now had my list of suspects down to four people to concentrate on, which was a lot better than twenty two!

About one in five of the trailers I passed had someone in

the yard, mowing. I recognized a few and waved.

It was really right there driving over to the Kocsis place where the obvious hit me right between the eyes and I knew who killed Bonnie Patrick. If I'd added the things we had up right I would have seen it from the very first. That was what the nagging was about. Now I had to find the motive and some way to prove it. I could easily show a very clear circumstantial case, but I couldn't bring one real shred of proof to a courtroom.

It had to be. It's the only way it added up.

I decided to go ahead with what I had planned, simply because eliminating all the others definitely would save time and trouble in a courtroom. Without something more solid to tie it, there couldn't be a conviction. I *must* have that motive!

Bill Kocsis wasn't home. He was at work. Wasn't it all too terrible, though that Patrick woman deserved a whole lot worse, if everything they said about her was true! If *half* of it was true!

"Mrs. Kocsis, I suppose a lot of it was true. Nobody looked at it from the point of view of Miss Patrick or from any perspective, except what they wanted to see."

"Oh, please! Call me Betty! Won't you come in? I was having a glass of orange juice with a little peach schnapps in it. It's very good, and not enough alcohol to affect you.

"Will you join me?"

I said I would like that, then she asked what I meant about not understanding.

"Miss Patrick was a famous artist. She painted under the name of Bonnie Bond. She was also not a particularly balanced person – mentally. She was schizophrenic, I think. She painted some of the finest nudes I've ever seen.

I've even arranged to buy one to hang in my Florida room. The subject is a friend of my wife and myself.

"She was ... I don't know how to explain it. She would find a man with the qualities she wanted in a model and would convince herself she was in love with him, then she'd paint him. It was like method acting. It wasn't the real Bonnie.

"I'm not explaining it well at all. I know that."

"You mean you bought a painting – of a nude – to hang in your Florida room?" she asked, looking at me somewhere between shocked and scandalized. "Something with lots of boobs for your wife to have to look at?"

"The model is a friend of ours named Mike Nelson. I want the painting because it's superb art. Alma agrees. Mike doesn't have boobs all over the place."

"It was a *male* nude?"

"Bonnie didn't paint female nudes, so far as I've found. She painted male nudes after she convinced herself she loved them. It shows. She did superb work. I'd buy most of her things, strictly for investment."

"I see! And what does your friend, the model, say? What happens when he comes over and sees the painting and everything hanging there?"

"He thinks she made him look sorta sexy. He doesn't realize he *is* sexy. He said it embarrasses him just a little because he knows Alma, but it doesn't bother him.

"Betty, this is *art*! It's not some porno crap! I think you should go over and look at the painting, sometime. You'd change your mind about Bonnie, I think. If you met Mike, I'm sure you would. She was a lot more than anyone here gave her credit for being."

"I didn't think you'd been around here long enough to

have your own affair with her. I guess all she needed was a day or two, though.

"You have to realize, she had a fling with Bill. I can't just forget that!"

"If you saw the paintings, you *would* forget it. I think you'd see what she was doing and I think you'd understand she wasn't ever any threat. She didn't want to take your husband, she just wanted to know him well enough to paint him. Her reaction to wives was because she couldn't understand what they were so afraid of. She really wasn't interested in taking anybody's husband."

"Then she painted Bill? He actually *posed* for her to paint him?"

"No, he didn't pose. A pose looks like a pose. It doesn't say anything. She wanted to capture the essence of the subject. Maybe she went about it the wrong way. Maybe it wasn't necessary for her to convince herself she loved the subject, but I don't think she would have been one tenth as good an artist if she didn't. It was her method. I think you should see some of her work, then you could make your own conclusions."

"I don't want to see any picture of my husband hanging in a gallery for everyone to gawk at! I don't want any nude pictures of him to be hanging anywhere!"

"I don't think you *should* see your husband's picture. Not yet, anyhow. I think it would be a shock to most women to see how another woman looked at her husband. I think you should see her work, then you could make your own conclusion as to how she might have painted him. I think maybe you'd find you didn't really feel at all negatively toward her, if you did.

"I better go. I have things to do. Anytime you want to see

her work, go over to the house and have Alma show you Mike's picture and some photos we have of him."

"What about Mike's wife? What does she say about the picture?"

"Mike's not married. I wouldn't consider hanging a married man's painting where his wife would see it. I think his girlfriend will think the painting is truly beautiful.

"You see, Betty, no one was threatened or even could imagine herself to be threatened, in Mike's case. I think you'll see you were never threatened by Bonnie if you go look at that painting. You'll see what it was really about."

She hummed and hawed, but I was sure she'd be over to see the painting pretty soon. I'd arrange with Alma about that. It was going to be interesting.

Now Helen Keene and Pat Schultz. Jim Tooney had seen his. He didn't have a wife to involve herself in the silly emotionalism.

If I *had* known Bonnie and she *had* painted me I wonder what Alma would do.

No I don't. Alma and I are secure in each other. She'd want to see if Bonnie saw in me what she sees in me. She'd probably want to buy the thing. Trouble is, if Bonnie didn't paint anyone she didn't sleep with, there wouldn't ever be such a painting of me. Alma would forgive me, but I wouldn't!

Chapter five

My next stop was Pat Schultz. It went much like the interview with Betty Kocsis. I suggested she and Norm could come over that evening to view the painting and just so we could get better acquainted.

She said she didn't much want to see anything Bonnie Patrick painted, but I convinced her to open her mind just a little and to be objective. When I promised I wasn't going to show any pictures of anyone in the immediate area, only one of a close friend from Englewood, she said they'd be over.

Helen Keene was enthusiastic, saying a friend in New York had told her about the painting of Steve on the marble bench. She admitted to being a little proud that her own husband was someone people would like to see in a painting, even a nude study. She was more than a little disappointed when I explained I wasn't showing any pictures of anyone they would know, just Mike.

She said they'd be over, and I used her phone to call Betty Kocsis to invite her, too, saying several people would be there for the same purpose. Everyone knew they had known Bonnie and even had those negative stories circulated about them, as had her own husband. She said they'd be there.

Just because I wanted to, I called on Sean and Lorna McMullin and Mac to invite them. Lorna grinned and said she'd like to see something Bonnie painted. Sean said he wasn't sure it was such a good idea to show a bunch of women a painting of a naked man.

"Sean, I think you'll agree the painting's in good taste," I replied. "This isn't some porn show. It's really art. I think most people had the wrong idea about Bonnie, but I also know it was her own fault. I think Lorna's gonna wish Bonnie'd painted one of you. We all get older and saggier. She's gonna someday wish she had a painting of you as you are now."

"So? She can take a picture with the Polaroid," Sean suggested with a grin.

"That ain't like art," Mac said. "I think I want to see what kind of stuff she did. I'm a little hotheaded, at times. Maybe I was a bit miffed she didn't want a tumble with me!"

We joked a bit, then I went back to the police station to see if there was anything new and to pick up blowups of the photos. I had the lab make a few quick blowup copies of some of the art I knew no one would know the subjects of.

"Dan thinks he's run down where she was from eleven thirty or so until one," Sam said. "It makes us one hell of a mess, though. She left the Bantam Strut Bar at one with a guy called Pete Mitchell. Dan's trying to run him down.

"Tom and Jean Billings lived in Maryland for seven or eight years before coming here, but there's no evidence they knew or ever heard of Bonnie there.

"Did you know about Pat Schultz coming from New York? Upstate, not the city. Norm met her while working there, then they moved to Pennsylvania, then here. They never were in New York at the same time as Bonnie and none of their friends ever heard of her. That all carries the tag line, `That we know of,' you'll understand.

"That's the crop until Dan can either eliminate Pete Mitchell or put him in the spotlight as a suspect."

"I'm having a get-together at the house tonight to show the wives of our suspects here the painting of Mike. I know who the murderer is. Now I have to find the motive."

"Who?" Sam asked.

"I can't say, for several reasons, but you have all the facts. It's pretty plain, if you look at it right. I just can't tie anything up! I don't see why she was killed at all!"

"It has something to do with that album?"

"It has to, but I can't see what. It's something that's as plain as the rest of it, but I seem to keep missing it. It doesn't make any sense. It's there to be seen, but I can't see it. I'm going to have to study those photos until I know where every speck of dust is. I want all the lists of everything found at the studio house and at her trailer. I want copies of all the pictures of those places.

"I'm asking, not demanding, whatever it sounds like."

"I'll have to send you a bill. The county's not going to approve using our labs for your benefit, you know. I'm already getting some heat from one of the commissioners. That tells us somebody's more worried about you than about me, but I have to watch it."

"Bill me whatever it costs. I thought that was understood from the first. In Englewood, Len Stewart always bills me for stuff the agency requests. I should've made that plain from the first."

"You gave them that forensic's lab that's better than anything in the rest of the state! They still charge you?"

"Len's got to answer to that county, too. I don't worry about costs. Cripes! It's good to have a little something to spend some of that money on. It doesn't accomplish a damned thing, sitting in the bank."

"I guess so. I don't know if I'll be over tonight. It depends on several things."

We talked a bit more, then I went home with the photos and locked myself in the upstairs study to pour over the pictures. I listed every least thing.

It would probably be of no use to list anything not directly connected with the murderer, but I couldn't know that. It was altogether possible she was murdered because of something in a painting of someone else or for something in a background photo that didn't appear to have anything to do with him.

The first one of Tooney had him on the beach. I listed the shells, the sea oats and all that stuff, but it was obvious from the start there was nothing in that painting. Background photo didn't have anything in it, either. No people way off, no odd boats, nothing on the beach, not even a telltale shadow that was out of place.

I went directly to the second picture of Tooney and listed everything starting from the far left top and moving toward the right. There was a picture of a sailing ship on a stormy sea on the wall. Down from that and to the right was the corner of a door frame. Next was a little end table with a lamp made from a green one gallon wine bottle with a brown burlap shade. The arm of the couch covered the lamp base and anything that was on the end table. The couch was brown leather, three large cushions – probably one of those things that fold out into a bed. There was a denim jacket with a Harley Davidson logo, worn and faded, on the back to the left, and a white bath towel to the right of it on the back. There were two magazines on the right end cushion – Hot Rod and Jugs. There was another end table with a lamp like the other one, a dirty orange ashtray, a digital clock that showed six seventeen with the little red light on – so it was probably taken in the afternoon, if Tooney bothered with such details. The coffee table in front of the couch was low, dark mahogany colored, and had a TV Guide, Two Penthouse (June and July, 1988. I could read the dates in the blowup), the TV remote control, a Field and Stream, a can of beer, an old motorcycle catalog, several water rings on the surface, and some CD disks and cartons.

I checked the painting and noted the Penthouse was the July issue, copied exactly, the TV Guide was the same, the beer can was the same brand and the Field and Stream was exact. The catalog was from 1985. Bonnie Bond didn't miss a detail. The fact the photo was taken at six seventeen, probably in July 1988, may be important.

I took a magnifying glass to look at the TV Guide, which I couldn't quite make the date out on, but I could find it from the picture, if it was important.

I checked everything one last time, then picked up the next picture from the stack, which was Norm Schultz. I located the background photo and checked it over, then listed the lamps, the inkmat, the stock certificates, the pictures and their frames, the jewelry case, the leather chairs, the bookcase, the desk, the photos on the walls, the silver trophies, the pen and pencil set, the grandfather clock, and the desk calendar. The date on that calendar was August 16, 1984.

That stopped me for a few seconds, but there was no reason to believe the background photo wasn't taken years before and kept in the box until she found a subject for it.

I got the magnifying glass out and minutely studied the photo. The pictures on the desk were of Schultz, Pat and two kids.

I sat back to think, then shook my head. So she knew Norm the year before she moved here. She'd been in his study room or den or whatever.

Maybe it was an office. I carefully studied the photo with the glass, but there wasn't any other clue until I checked the few titles I could read in the bookcase. It was legal crap. Corporate law, securities law, and various other legal precedent studies.

Had Norm been a lawyer? Had he been a corporate lawyer with a lot of ambition, which Bonnie depicted very well in her painting?

I knew that Norm killed her. That was obvious from the start – or should have been. Nothing else fit.

It had to be something connected to her knowing him before she or he moved down to Florida. It also had to be something in that photo! I had the answer in my hands right then – and couldn't see it!

I checked the picture of the painting again. The only obvious differences in the items in the background photo was that the emerald and diamond necklace he was holding up in the painting was just barely showing in the jewelry case in the photo and things had been moved around for effect, though they were exact, except for that rearrangement.

Crap! New York, here I come! There was no way around it. I had to somehow find his motive so I could face him with the fully accomplished solution to the case. I didn't want him to have any way out. He could just grin his friendly grin at me now. I couldn't hope to touch him. Hell, if it was something from '84 I probably couldn't, anyhow. Statute of limitations.

The answer was in New York. I was sure of it.

I went to tell Alma I was going, then called Mike Nelson and asked him to get the jet ready. I got a bright idea and asked if he'd like to come to the house tonight. He said he'd fly his old Piper Cub down and would bring Annette, his girlfriend. I told him his picture was hanging in the Florida room, he said she'd probably get a kick out of it. I could picture him immediately blushing.

I grinned to myself and called Selma to invite her to join us. I didn't tell her Mike would be there.

Mike and Annette came in a little after Lorna, Sean, and Mac arrived. Alma decided we'd wait until everyone was there to go in to see the painting, so we had some coffee and cognac while we waited. Lorna kept looking at Mike in a speculative way, which made him blush a couple of times.

Annette was as fresh and natural as Shirley Bock or Mike, and was a natural beauty, herself.

Sean was a little uncomfortable at first, but soon warmed to Mike and was much more at ease. He even made a little joke or two about the painting and asked Mike if he really minded that everyone was going to be seeing him in the altogether in a little while.

"I guess you can see as much when I'm in my regular cutoffs. I think the only thing that's any different is that Bonnie made me look so sexy, and I'm not that way. It's sort of exciting."

"You may not *know* you're sexy, but you definitely *are*!" Lorna said, which drew a deep blush from Mike.

Norm, Pat, Bill, and Betty all arrived next, followed in about five minutes by Steve, Helen and Selma. We all went into the living room for coffee and cognac and for those of us already having drinks to finish ours, then we went on into the Florida room. The women had been studying Mike all along, but Selma had given it away when she said he looked exactly like the painting, except for the sexy look on his face. The painting still got a strong reaction from everybody.

"It *is* sort of good, isn't it?" Mike asked.

"It's fabulous!" Annette cried.

"It's completely different from what I pictured her doing," Sean said. "It's not at all.... It's really good. I agree."

"I see what you meant about Bonnie," Mac said. "She really was a good artist, wasn't she?"

"I think I see, too," Helen agreed. "Oh, I wish I had that painting of Steve!"

"You *know* about that?!" Steve cried.

"Shawna told me about it," Helen explained. "She saw it in a gallery in New York."

"Which one?" Steve asked.

"I don't know," Helen replied. "Those New York art galleries all have weird names."

"He meant which painting," Norm said. "I think Bonnie did two or three of them with Steve as subject."

So he was going to try to draw the attention away from himself by causing trouble between others, was he?

Not even maybe!

"I saw those she made of you," I noted, innocently. "The first one was done years ago, wasn't it?"

He turned red and said he didn't know if she made more than one of him. Pat looked disgusted, but then said she didn't really mind, if the paintings were as tasteful and as downright *good* as this one was! Betty said I had been right that she would have liked to have a painting of her husband like that, but she didn't think she would want it out for everyone to see.

"Really? Why not?" Bill asked. "I think it would be a real hoot! I never saw the one she did of me. I'm sure she didn't do more than one. We really didn't care that much for each other. She thought I was too concerned with things and I thought she was a bit of a bitch."

"Well, your painting shows she thought you were sort of selfcentered," Alma said. "She thought Steve was a very studious man, in private. She saw Norm as wanting material things. She saw Jim Tooney almost as a sort of god, at first, but she later saw him as just a typical male chauvinist pig.

"I didn't see the actual paintings, but I saw photos of them. She was a very good artist. I wish she'd painted CD."

"I think I wish she'd painted Sean," Lorna said. "CD said I'd feel that way after I saw her work."

"I had her pegged all wrong," Mac apologized. "I thought she was a two-bit whore on the make for anything in pants, but she was doing it all for the art, wasn't she? She was in love with Mike, here, when she painted that. It shows. She saw him as a sort of Earth god. That has to make a man feel good!"

Mike blushed and Annette said she wished she had some talent, because she saw Mike exactly like in that painting, which made him blush more.

Selma said she understood that some people changed, like Tooney did over the years, to Bonnie, while some stayed the same.

"Steve didn't change one bit to her," Alma agreed. "I think there's one of him at the studio house isn't there, CD?

Maybe Helen would want to bid on it, but they won't sell them cheap!"

"How much did you have to pay for me, CD?" Mike asked.

"Twelve and a half."

"You should have gotten two at that price!" Mike said. "For twenty five hundred bucks, you could have sold me one!"

"Twelve thousand five hundred," Alma said.

"Oh, jeez! I don't think I'm worth *that* much!"

"I'll give you twenty thousand for that one, right now!" Selma said.

"Hey!" Mike yelled.

"Bid! I'll give you twenty two five," Lorna countered.

"Hey!" Mike yelled.

"Do I hear twenty five?" I asked.

"Hey!" Mike yelled.

"It's not for sale!" Alma said. "I come in here and look at it, then go into the bedroom with CD where it's dark and I can fantasize...."

"Hey!" Mike yelled. "Cut it out! That's not fair!"

Lorna giggled and we all teased Mike, who really loved it. He blushed so much that night I was afraid he'd become permanently beet red.

When everyone went home, they had a very different opinion of Bonnie Bond. Alma and I were a lot closer to the McMullins and the Keenes, and were also were a little closer to Betty Kocsis and Pat Schultz, but Bill would never be close to anyone and Norm must have had some suspicions that I had him figured.

Tomorrow, I was flying to New York. Maybe Norm had good reason to worry. Maybe I'd find my motive there.

"CD? Sam here," woke me as I picked up the phone.

"What? You got something?"

"Two little things. Number one, Bonnie left Pete at two or thereabout and he went off with a couple of friends to try to pick up some broads at the beach thing. Norman Schultz called to say he'd been approached by some anonymous voice who said he'd better come up with ten grand or his wife would get certain photos. Seeing as we found the album and there aren't any such pictures out there to blackmail anyone with, I see why you must have decided he did it. I thought you'd want to know.

"How did your party go?"

"I sort of hinted I might know something, so Norm called you with that to try to divert my suspicion. He's not dangerous to anyone else for a little while, so don't do anything to worry him. I'm off on a little trip today. I hope to be able to come back tonight or tomorrow, at the latest, with what I need, then we can arrange a little meeting to close this one up."

"Were we right? Was it something in the photo album?"

"To tell the truth, I really don't know for certain. It has to be, but I'm not sure what it could be. He searched for that album for a reason.

"Did you know Norm was once a corporate lawyer?"

"He worked for one in Buffalo, but I don't know if he was a lawyer himself. Pat was a legal secretary and got him the job with the firm when he was laid off where they were living in Detroit. They have two kids, one's nineteen and one's twenty, both married. They had the first when they were married about four months. She was sixteen and he was seventeen. They had the next one year and a couple of months later. They stayed with an aunt and uncle on

Norm's side ,in Buffalo, when Norm and Pat moved here.

"Norm worked at the union in Detroit for about four years and learned the legal end of that. They saved up a lot of money and moved to Buffalo, New York, where she was raised, when the job market went to hell in Detroit in seventy four, then they went back to Detroit when things picked up, then back to New York when things got to the unstable point, late in eighty two. Pat took a job right away, and they seemed to live very frugal lives for about a year, then he went to work with the firm. Soon they were throwing money around.

"I learned all of this stuff direct from the IRS. They were already investigating him because of the money he had on hand, but couldn't find any irregularities. It was barely possible they had slowly saved a lot of money over the years. He spread the word he won a bundle in a poker game, but they couldn't run it down. The wife said he had saved twenty dollars or more a week in a steel box in their garage for the whole eighteen years they were married when the IRS investigation took place, three years ago. That would give them about twenty grand to throw around. They've thrown more than that around, but nothing can be proved about it.

"They accounted for the money to buy that place at the trailer court by selling their place in Buffalo that her parents left her when they died in that big train wreck in Canada in eighty one. They've spent more than that, but nothing that can't be explained away.

"Norm bought that Cadillac they drive for cash. Nobody has a clue about where it came from. There are other cash purchases."

"Seems you did quite a neat little job on them, didn't

you?"

"I did quite a little job on all of them. We're in the era of the computer. I punch buttons and get a printout. I don't have to check in person – which is maybe what you should do."

"The thing I need isn't in any computer. It's hidden in the past and in those photos and paintings. I have to be there to put the various pieces where they belong. I'll be in touch as soon as I get back."

I was awake, so I got up, saw it was five thirty AM, grinned and went to the bathroom to clean up and dress. Alma got up while I was packing a small suitcase (I keep plenty of clothes on the Jet, but I only use those if I have to) and made breakfast. I got in the Trans Am and drove up I-75 to Sarasota and to the airport. Shirley Bock-Jacobi greeted me and handed me my keys to the jet, I chatted a few minutes, then I was off.

I was landing in Buffalo three hours later, having used the time in flight to study things while the autopilot did most of the flying. I decided the first thing I had to do was find where Bonnie and Norm met in 1984. I could work from there, but I had to have a base.

"Mr. Norman and Patricia Schultz?" the efficient receptionist at Burkhart, Burns, Evans, Cromwell and Smith asked, as she studied the appointment list. "Norman and Patricia Schultz? I'll have to check the records and get an official authorization to distribute any information from the board.

"Could you tell us why you desire the information?"

"I'm an investigator working with the State of Florida on a murder case. The information may be critical to that investigation."

She mumbled into a phone and an older man with white hair and (Yes!) pence-nez came out to ask me into his office.

"Mr. Cromwell, Mr. Grimes," the receptionist said, and went back to her typewriter.

"What's this thing I heard about Norman Schultz being murdered?" Cromwell asked.

"He wasn't the victim. We have to determine a great deal about the pasts of various people there, Pat and Norm among them. We have to particularly find where he first met the victim and the circumstances surrounding that meeting and other meetings."

"Are Mr. and Mrs. Schultz suspects?"

"You and I are suspects, unless and until we're definitely eliminated. Mr. Schultz had opportunity to kill the woman, but I'm not here to find out about that, now. It happened in Florida on the first. I've come here to investigate things that happened here back in eighty three and four."

"Besides you and me and Norman Schultz, are there any other major suspects?" he said with a grin. "I'm a lawyer. I want to know things before I'll give you any information."

"The major serious suspects, from the first, were Norm, a man named Steve Keene or his wife, Helen, William or Betty Kocsis, Selma Wentworth, Tom and Jean Billings, Jim Tooney, Paul, Winnie and Jennie Allen, and Sean, Lorna and Mac McMullins. Selma Wentworth and the McMullins group are completely cleared, at this point, unless there's something we don't yet know. I'm interested in clearing all suspects I can, because that's usually the fastest way to handle this type of investigation. Once we get this kind of case down to three or four suspects, we've as much as solved it, because little things start to add up."

"Who was the victim?"

"A woman called Bonnie Patrick, there."

"Doesn't ring any bells."

"She's better known here under the name of Bonnie Bond, an artist."

"I see where this is going, now. Candice has that painting the Bond woman made of Norman. You think that maybe Patricia didn't know about the paintings, found out, and killed her?"

"Pat is accounted for at the time of the murder. She is *not* a suspect. Which painting does Candice have? The one on the beach?"

"The one by the high mountain stream. She called it `Young Satyr' or something such. Candice had seen some of her work in a small gallery in New York and said it was good. She wanted one as an investment and she was a bit stuck on Norman at the time, so she commissioned Miss Bond to do a painting for her, using him as a model. It was all quite innocent, and the rest of it was simply stories and rumors. They didn't have an affair, if that's what you're after. Neither Norman and Candice nor Norman and Miss Bond. Patricia knew Norman was posing for a painting, but she never saw the work. Candice didn't have people who.... She never saw the work, but she knew he had posed for a nude painting.

"I believe Miss Bond and Norman met right here in Candice's office. Miss Bond went with Norman to a place out in the country, where she took a few Polaroid pictures of him in the setting and, so far as I was aware, never saw him again. If she was killed in Florida and Norman had opportunity, it becomes rather evident he saw her recently, there."

"Candice is?"

"Miss Candice Evans, a founding partner in this firm. If you wish to speak with her I'll see if she's free."

I nodded and he buzzed her office, then talked to her a few seconds. He hung up the phone and said I could go to her office, two doors to my left on the same side of the hall.

Candice Evans was obviously an attractive woman in her younger days. She was an attractive woman now, in her mid-fifties. She had me sit, finished signing a few papers, and soon asked what I wanted to know about Norman Schultz and/or Bonnie Bond. I told her about the murder and said Norman had been a model for several paintings and lived less than a quarter of a mile from her when she was killed, so we, quite naturally, had to deeply investigate everything about both of them.

"I have the painting she made of him and three of her fantasy landscapes. I suppose they'll be worth a fortune, now. She didn't do many landscapes.

"I saw her work in New York City and bought a small landscape. She was having a show and was exhibiting two classical-style nudes in it. I immediately saw they were as good as any I've ever seen and asked her if she would do a work on a prepaid commission contract. She said it depended on what I wanted, so I said I wanted whatever she could come up with. I said I'd supply the live model, she would paint him. She shrugged and said she'd come to meet the model and look for something she could say with a painting of him. If things clicked, she would do the painting for five thousand dollars. I had to give her five hundred to come here to see if she *would* paint him.

"I had a bit of a crush on Norman. I think it's best you know I did have a minor little affair with him for a short time, but I don't want that to become general knowledge. No one knows. It was more a fling than an affair.

"Bonnie painted the scene for me, as agreed. She told me after they came back from the place where she took the pictures she wouldn't do a nude man unless she'd first bedded him. She said she would do the painting for me as agreed. She said the place in the painting had special meaning to her, so I knew she found the spot and laid him right there, then took her working photos. I saw one of the pictures and was very much interested in seeing the painting. Here's a picture."

She took an eight by ten from her desk drawer and handed it to me. It was Norm standing by a little stream with his foot up on a log, bending to put his elbow on his knee and resting his chin on his fist. He was looking toward the viewer and slightly upward left. The look on his face was amused and inviting at the same time. You had the feeling he had that split second looked up to see someone watching him. It was as good as her other work. The little "B.B." was in the corner.

"She captured him very well, didn't she?" Candice asked. "I mean, he loves nothing more in the world than a tumble in the hay, but he's a little irresponsible about it. He's basically interested in being satisfied, himself, without giving a hot damn if his partner is.

"I mean, the look she got on his face! It's like he's about to say, `Hi, there! Wanna hava quickie?' That's Norman! She extracted his very essence and put it on canvas!"

"I think she had a strong native ability to do that with all the men she painted. There's no doubt, whatever, about the type of person a man was when she painted him."

"Are you saying he changed, or is it about someone else?"

"Her later paintings of him leaned toward a greedier more acquisitive nature and put his sexuality down on the list a good way. She could paint a nude in such a way my wife says any woman looking at the work will know that's not the man they want to know. There's one we know who Alma says is like a pretty trinket. He doesn't do anything for the work. He's there, but so what? He's completely empty and totally void of any socially redeeming features."

"And in person?" she asked, smiling slightly at me.

"He's a yuppie who's completely empty and who has no socially redeeming features. He's an original suspect, but I doubt such a person is capable of this kind of murder. They can't do anything that would make such a strong statement. If they kill anyone, it's generally some kind of ploy to grab some headlines or something."

We talked a minute more, then I left. It was something, but it wasn't enough. It didn't connect anything in the painting or the photo except the fact he had worked at the firm and had had an affair with Candice *and* Bonnie in '83 and '84. Candice wasn't a suspect. Everybody knew he'd had a bit of an affair with her then, they just didn't know it was such a longterm thing. There was more – and I had to find it!

Chapter six

Where to now? I'd found out a whole hell of a lot more than I had thought, but it wasn't enough. It did leave me wondering if maybe Pat knew about the killing and was even a part of it. Did she get deliberately drunk so it would make Norm's drunk act more effective? She knew he posed for a painting back in '83.

OK. Maybe she'd been stewing about living so close to Bonnie for a long time and had joined him in a plot to kill her. It still left us with the fact that it WAS him who did it, and there was still nothing that would serve as a motive strong enough for him to have killed her. There was something missing. I'd flown all the way to Buffalo, New York, for nothing, really. This bit of background could be found over the phone in ten minutes.

No. It was worth it. We could never have gotten that story over the phone. We could have surmised he'd slept with her, simply because that was her style when painting, but we couldn't know about his affair with Candice.

I decided to go to the gallery to see what the plan was. That meant going into New York, which I wasn't thrilled about, but what the hell.

Maharajhahzi's Gallery of Fine Art is on a side street in a very plush setting. It's one of those places you might find by accident if you were walking along the street, but it catered to serious collectors and announced its sales and shows to a select clientele. I introduced myself to the proprietor, who said to call him Yagob. I explained I was investigating the Bond murder and he asked when the stuff was going to be released. I told him I should have the case wrapped up in a few days – if I could get a break.

He showed me a catalog of all of Bonnie's works he had sold or still had on hand. I bought a copy of the work and paid for the painting of Mike. He then showed me the other paintings he had in the gallery for sale, one of which was Steve Keene. It showed him reclining on a chaise lounge by a marble pool. The view was from the foot of the lounge and to his right. There was a glass of iced tea and a large pink Phalaenopsis orchid on a little wrought iron table beside him. He had one arm behind his head and was staring into space, a rapt look on his face. He had the near leg slightly raised at the knee. The hand on his free arm was holding a paperback copy of Isaac Asimov's *Foundation and Empire* on the table.

I almost expected a stray breeze to make the orchid spray wave slightly. The detail work was perfect. The price on it was seventy five hundred. I bought it. It was as good as the one of Mike, and I liked Helen and Steve. I knew she'd love that painting!

There was nothing else at the gallery, then. Yagob couldn't tell me anything that wasn't in the catalog. He knew her from her shows, but they hadn't been close. It was strictly a business deal. He was going to become very wealthy, now that she was dead, but he would have much preferred to make the money more slowly through a continuing supply of her work.

I thought of stopping in Maryland on the way home, but Jean and Tom Billings weren't part of this murder, so whatever they had to hide could stay hidden. I had a painting to make a gift of and a few facts that would help fill out the life story of Bonnie Patrick, but I still didn't have my motive. All I had was the circumstantial parts I had all along.

I got back to Sarasota at seven fifteen in the evening. Mike and Annette were at the hangar and Shirley Bock came out of the office. I unwrapped the painting and showed it to them. That led to me finding the photo of the one of Mike to show Shirley, which made Mike blush all over.

Then to the Trans Am and home!

"CD, we can't accept this!" Steve said. "It's more than we could ever afford, and we simply can't accept gifts that are so expensive."

"Don't be silly!" Alma argued. "You know full well CD owns the Crane plants. He can't possibly spend even a sizable percent of all the money that comes in, even while he's asleep. If he wants you to have the thing, take it!"

"It's truly magnificent!" Helen exclaimed. "I was so *wrong* about Bonnie! I thought she was so shallow, but she could see exactly what I see in Steve! You know very well I can't turn this down, don't you?"

"Of course I know it," Alma agreed. "I *said* I wished she'd painted one of CD. She was a truly superb artist. It's such a shame about her."

"Can I call Selma?" Helen asked.

"Certainly! Have her come over here. Alma can throw a little lunch together and we can visit awhile before I get back on the case. I need to relax and try to find another perspective on this mess. I'm in a rut I can't seem to get out of."

Helen called Selma and she and Connie came over a few minutes later. Helen showed them the painting. She was obviously proud of it.

"I'll say one thing about Bonnie," Connie finally said. "She was damned good! It looks exactly like Steve."

"I think she captured something extraordinary in everything she did, didn't she?" Selma asked. "She caught Mike's innocence, while making him so sexy, and she caught Steve's quiet sexuality. With Mike you could have a wild, passionate, fun time, but with Steve, you'd feel safe and protected."

"Who's Mike?" Connie asked, so we had to show her the painting in the den. She said she'd never forgive us for having him there and not having her over, so we told her we were saving her for Jim, who Bonnie never painted.

Alma fixed us all Cajun fried popcorn shrimp and a crab salad. We had a very relaxing two hours, then I went over to the police station to talk with Sam. He hadn't found anything new and I gave him a full report on what I'd found. I showed him the art catalog and we went through it. Other than showing she knew Norm since '83, there wasn't anything new in it.

"Damn it, Sam! We're overlooking something obvious! I know it! His motive's staring us in the face, and has been, all along. We seem to refuse to see it, for some reason!

"I don't mean some silly explosion of passion after all this time or anything like that. I mean a rock-solid motive. It must have something to do with all the money he seemed to have that wasn't accounted for, but I can't see what it could be."

"Maybe he embezzled something from the lawyers' firm?"

"No. Cromwell made it plain there was no complaint against either Norm or Pat. If there was anything at all they would have been all over me to hang his ass. It would damage the reputation of their old and trusted firm.

"He couldn't have been blackmailing her! She wasn't the type who could *be* blackmailed."

"Maybe he was involved in something in Detroit? We could be concentrating on the wrong place."

"It would have to be something that happened since he met her in eighty three. He has all that money that still has to be explained, somehow.

"I wonder if he still has a lot of money? He bought the Caddy and some other expensive items for cash."

"He and Pat don't make that kind of money working around that trailer park. I suppose he has his stash somewhere. Maybe she found it?"

"And he thought she might be carrying it around with her?" I said. "I still think it's the album he was searching for. It's something in that album that's our clue to his motive."

We went through the catalog very carefully one more time, but there wasn't anything there, so we went over the album and the photos.

"It's there. It has to be there. I overlooked the obvious from the start or we wouldn't have wasted time on most of the others. I'm overlooking something.... what about those jewels? She painted the exact thing she saw, so she had that necklace to look at. Maybe it was stolen?"

"How could we find out? It was six years ago.

"I don't see how he would kill her for painting the necklace, anyhow. He could always claim he didn't know where it came from. He thought it belonged to a client at the law firm or he could claim he never saw it before and didn't know where she got it. By itself, it doesn't tell us much."

"But with her testimony?

"It's all I see right now, so I'm going to try to find out about it. If it *was* stolen, maybe she found he had stolen.... Why would she wait until now? What happened the last few days of last year that would bring it to mind? She painted it six years ago, as you say.

"Damn it! I just don't see any other possible connection!"

"Why would he kill her if it was a stolen necklace and she knew it? She wouldn't try to blackmail him, surely. She would either call the police on him or forget about it."

"It's all I have. I'll spend a little more time on it. Maybe she told him she wanted an explanation or she was going to the police and any investigation would turn up a lot more than a necklace."

"It hasn't," he pointed out.

"We haven't looked at it from that angle. It's all I have. I have to do something with it."

"See if you can locate where he's hidden his cash stash. I can tell you it's not in any bank and it's not in CDs or other investments I can discover."

"That would be part of it. I'll be in touch."

I went out to sit in the Jeep a minute, then went home and called Cromwell. He said the firm did not, now, nor had it ever, kept jewelry or anything such for clients, and would not keep any such items at the firm if they did. I thanked him and sat back to think.

I was going about this all wrong. There had to be some way she found out about stolen jewels and connected it with Norm. If it was jewels stolen six years ago it wasn't likely she would have panicked him enough for him to kill her. If he got the money for the jewels she wouldn't be able to prove anything, and she damned well couldn't prove the necklace in her painting was the stolen piece. It *wasn't* showing in the photo. It was in that box and out of sight.

Off on a tangent again, but there wasn't anything else to do with this one. If it was over something that happened six years ago, necklace or something else, it was going to be very hard to prove any connection.

She was killed and searched. Her trailer was also searched.

She had hidden the album.

She showed the album to prospective models.

There was something in that album that was deadly serious to the killer.

The photos were all that was in the album. There was nothing hidden anywhere in disappearing ink or anything and there wasn't any code, other than the one on the photos that attached them with the painting.

I took out my copies of the photos and studied the code a few minutes. A-4, L-9 and L-10. Not anything that could be decoded, if it was in that. There was nothing to act as reference point. That would leave it useless to ever prove anything.

I drove over to the Keene's place and looked across the road at the Schultz place. That was right and fit only one way. Both Pat and Norm were at work, so I walked around and looked at the other people in the area, working in their lawns and visiting one another.

Sam said Pat reported Norm kept the money in a steel box in the garage, but they only had a carport here and there was no place for a steel box.

There was a vacant lot behind the Schultz trailer. No one appeared to be home in the home to one side. There was a sign on the vacant lot saying it was for sale. I strolled casually across and into Norm's back yard. There was an aluminum shed on the back end of the carport slab with a locked door. There was a ventilation vent high in back. I found a loose concrete block and stood on it to look in. A washer and dryer, bleach, detergent, laundry basket and that sort of thing. No steel box I could see.

There was another shed built on the side of the mobile home by the rear door. It didn't have any lock. I opened the door and looked in. Lawnmower, hoses, fertilizer and spreader, sprinklers, shovel, hoe, rake, – and all this for a ten by twenty eight foot stretch of grass in back and a few plants along the sides and in front. No steel box.

I went back out to the road and around to my Jeep. If he had a strongbox it would be inside and in a closet. That's where anyone would want to keep a strongbox. I wasn't into breaking and entering, so I drove over to the pool area to check out the crime scene one more time. I had to be right, there. Nothing had changed my mind in any way. It was Norm. I needed the motive and I had him.

Next stop was in front of Bonnie's trailer to sit and go over the place in my mind. I had a thought and got out to go around by the kitchen door to look in the garbage can still sitting there. The parts of the pages cut from the encyclopedia were there, so she'd made that hiding place recently. She'd never hidden the album before. It was something she just discovered and she knew it may be important to hide it.

There was a shoebox-size carton and one a bit larger under the encyclopedia sheets. The Scotch tape that had been holding the lids on was dark caramel in color, so it was at least three years old. There were some receipts from 1977 through 1984 in the can and some canceled checks and bank statements from the same time period.

Another little piece fell into place, then. She was going through some old papers she saved when she moved down to Florida. Most of them were out of date, so she threw them out, then she came across something. It caught her attention, then she remembered something in her photo album. She got it out and there it was! It had been Norman Schultz who stole those jewels! She had the proof in her painting!

Maybe there was a simple explanation. Maybe it was the wrong necklace. She would face Norm with it – but she'd better hide the evidence, because she was safe, so long as she had it. She just didn't realize the evidence wouldn't mean a thing to anyone who didn't know what they were looking for.

She faced him with it, he agreed to meet her at the pool, he killed her.

Why did he agree to meet her at the pool?

Because Pat didn't know anything about it and he couldn't talk to Bonnie at my party. He would explain everything, later. Pat would sleep like a log after a couple of drinks and would never know he was gone. It wasn't really him, it was John Doe, a friend of his. He was only covering for him, but there's no time to talk. Someone will see and will run to Pat.

Then why did she hang around?

She really didn't have anywhere else to go. When it became obvious she wasn't going to be the center of attention at that party, she went to another one.

No. He would talk to her later when he could be sure they wouldn't be seen. It wasn't him, it was blah, blah, blah. Then he couldn't get anywhere near her to discuss it, so he agreed to meet her at the pool when Pat was home and passed out, so she left. That was more likely. How it was done wasn't the problem. The motive was the problem. Bonnie had left it for us to find.

Maybe that wouldn't be too hard to do! It was worth a shot!

I went straight home and grabbed the phone and the picture of the painting, then got the NYC police department and gave them a little spiel about working on a murder case and being a state grand jury investigator. I told the operator I would have to speak with an expert on missing property and was connected with a Sgt. Klein.

"This isn't going to be easy. I'm looking at a picture I'll have to use to describe an item. It would be part of a major heist in eighty three or four."

"I can put it into the computer as you describe it. We'll see what comes out," Klein suggested.

"Its an emerald and diamond necklace. I can see four square-cut emeralds, about three quarters of an inch on a side. There are smaller diamonds surrounding the large emeralds. The setting looks like heavy gold."

"Mmm. Can you count the exact number of diamonds around one of the large emeralds?"

"Five to a side, sharing the corners. Sixteen around each emerald. I'd estimate maybe half a carat apiece."

"Is there a teardrop-shaped emerald, large, on the end of the chain of emeralds and diamonds?"

"Not that I can see."

"Then it's probably the Hansington stuff. It was stolen from the Arnold Hansington Penthouse on April ninth, nineteen eighty three, between three and four in the morning. The safe was drilled and the chest of jewels, including the item you describe and three quarters of a million more in jewels, were taken. The necklace was worth half a million in itself. There were a lot of papers and bonds stolen at the same time."

"I see. I'll let you know if this turns out to be anything to get something out of your records for you. I guess the statue of limitations would put the thieves out of reach of the law in a couple of months."

"Nah! The thieves killed Arnold Hansington when they cracked the safe. There's no limitation on murder! If you find anything, we get first crack at it!"

"I think the thief committed a murder here. You can have him after he fries."

We talked a minute, then I hung up.

If she could tie him tightly to that necklace she could tie him to the murder – and *that* was motive aplenty! My only problem was going to be how to solidly tie him to the necklace, now that Bonnie was dead and couldn't testify as to where she got the necklace she painted him holding.

The next call was to Sam, who I told about the whole thing. He said he'd wait to grab Norm. We couldn't prove anything, yet, as I so thoughtfully pointed out. We had the circumstantial and we had the money he was spending, but a jury would let him go, ninety percent of the time, for that kind of evidence. It was pure speculation. We needed something more than just knowing we were right. We had to be able to prove it, beyond a reasonable doubt, in a court of law.

I was going to do that! One way or another, I was going to tag that one!

I suddenly grabbed for the phone again, called Sam and yelled for him to meet me at Bonnie's place in ten seconds at the very latest and hung up. I then made another quick call to NYCPD and talked to Klein. I wrote the information he gave – which I was sure would do it – then ran for the Jeep. Sam and Dan Ford arrived at Bonnie's ten minutes after I got there. We went inside, where I showed them the things we'd been overlooking all along. It had been right there in front of us and was even on my list of items in her house. We did a fast check, then Sam asked how I wanted to handle it.

"Just once in my life, I want to be able to do a real Nero Wolfe type of thing. I want to call all the people who were at my house to see Mike's picture over there and I want to present everything to them, then have you take the killer out."

"How will you handle it? I mean, can you be sure he'll come?" Dan asked.

"He won't dare refuse."

We took all the stuff we'd need. Sam would bring blow-ups of the pictures we'd want and everyone would meet at my place at seven sharp. I called them all to say I was going to expose the murderer tonight, and they were invited. Most were curious, so they said they'd be there. Pat said she'd be there and called to Norm off in the background. He said they might as well come. They didn't have any plans.

I felt a little sorry for Pat, but there was no way she didn't know about the theft and the money she'd helped spend, so she wasn't the great innocent, either.

I told Selma to invite Connie, if she liked.

It wasn't completely ready, of course. I had to get it ready, but was antsy as hell by the time everyone showed up. Alma seated all of them around the Florida room and

I made my grand entrance with Sam and Dan behind me. We were all three carrying the stuff we needed.

Very dramatic.

"This part shouldn't take too very long," I announced, when everyone was quiet. "I was able to solve the identity of Bonnie's killer fairly quickly. I should have seen it immediately, but I had to take the time to get the proof together.

"We'll first review events, then explain what happened and why.

"I'll start with the murder, itself. You can follow along and see who the murderer had to be.

"Bonnie Patrick came to a new year's party at my house. She made her general splash, drifted around, then left at a strange time. She was subsequently found dead at the pool in the trailer court recreation area. She had been struck on the forehead with a blunt object, stunning her, then she was strangled with a towel. Her body had been searched. We later determined her house had been searched.

"Bonnie Patrick came to a new year's party at my house for the sole purpose of talking to one of you about something she found, totally by accident, as she was going through old records. She asked that one to explain the things she'd discovered and was assured the explanation was to be forthcoming, but that person couldn't talk there with everyone watching her. She hung around, but there was no opportunity to talk then, thus an agreement was made to meet her later at the pool house.

"Bonnie Patrick was given a key to let her into the gate and another to let her into the changing room. She was a hedonist and decided to swim a bit, since she was there, anyhow. The fact she was meeting her killer didn't ever occur to her.

"Bonnie Patrick was killed and the keys removed from her body, she was searched, her clothing was searched, the killer wiped the lock on the gate clean after closing it and drove her car to her trailer, where another search was made. The item the killer searched for was not found. Sheriffs Dan Ford and Sam Lukens found that item (I held up the album).

"You can see who the killer had to be became more than obvious – if I didn't spot it immediately – at the pool house. It could only be one of three people, and we'd immediately eliminated one, Mrs. Bellows, because she wasn't anywhere around when she would have had to be."

"Obvious? How do you mean?" Connie asked.

"Who among you has keys to the gate and the dressing rooms?"

They first looked around at each other, then all of them looked at Selma, then at Norm. Pat gasped and jumped up, knocking over her chair.

"Pat, he kept giving you drinks and kept pouring them for himself, but nobody ever saw him drink anything. He pretended to be drunk so you'd give him an alibi. I came over the next day and you could barely navigate, but he was fine."

"That's ridiculous!" Norm said. "Why would I kill her?"

"Because she could put you on death row in New York for an old murder."

He grinned, and shook his head.

"Norm?" Pat squeaked.

"Did you know that he killed the man who owned the necklace and stocks?"

"That wasn't him! It was the man with him!"

"I don't know what you're talking about," Norm said. "Go ahead and get this farce over with. I'll be most happy to point out the holes in your theory, after I've heard it all."

"You know, I've heard fifty people say they don't know what I'm talking about at fifty different times and, as yet, not one was telling the truth. Onward!

"I will tell you it was a bad mistake to call Sam to report a blackmail attempt. It convinced him you were our guilty party. We'd found the album. I already said that. There was then nothing to use to blackmail anybody, ergo no black-mailing attempt, ergo you were lying to cover your own tail. That was immensely stupid.

"The trail was easy to follow. I went to New York, where I talked to Mr. Cromwell and Candice Evans. You posed for Bonnie in nineteen eighty three and started your affair with her then. A short time later you suddenly had a lot of money, after living frugally for more than a year. You said you had saved the money slowly over the years, yet you've spent more than you made in those years, recently. You got the money selling the jewels and stocks. Those stocks were in bearer blocks.

"You had to kill Bonnie and you had to get the photos of those stocks and bonds(I held up the enlarged photo of the desk). She had painted you with the emeralds (I held up the enlarged photo of the painting), but that wasn't enough – by itself – to prove anything. Those emeralds *and* the stock certificates would put you on death row.

"While you were searching for the album you passed right over the old newspapers on the end table by the bookcase (I held them up). Those papers were mainly concerned with art shows featuring her work, but there was a story next to one of her reviews that described the emerald necklace, the robbery and murder, and had a picture of that necklace, big as life! (I held that story up.)

"That story came out on April the fifth, which was a full year before she painted you with that necklace. She didn't even notice the article, at the time, but she was cleaning out old records when she happened across it. She had an eye for detail like no one else in the world.

"That was the necklace she used in the painting! It had been in that jewelry chest on your desk! (I held the photo up and pointed to the chest.) She had a picture of the desk with the chest sitting on it, but the emerald necklace wasn't visible in the photo. You could claim anything about the necklace, including that you'd never seen it before it showed up in that painting. The jewelry chest itself was a common enough type that it would be inconclusive in evidence. You were safe enough – there.

"What was conclusive evidence in the photo was this stack of stocks (Pointing to them in the photo). Those, along with the necklace, would end it for you.

"On that bunch of old newspapers was an old Forbes Magazine (I held it up, open to a story). In that magazine was a list of trading numbers of those same stock certif- icates. There are four of those numbers visible in the photo and copied exactly much larger in the painting (Pointing to them). You'd taken up with her again. I thought at first that had something to do with the murder, but you've been her lover a lot longer than Tooney. You were her lover since nineteen eighty three. The fact Pat came home to find her across the street was a bit suspicious, at the time, then I realized people who work on their yards and their visitors always park on the same side of the street as the trailer – not across the street. Pat came home and almost caught the two of you together.

"Surprisingly enough, that caused me to waste some time on a blind trail.

"Now, you can refute anything you disagree with."

He looked at Sam and Dan to either side of him and said, "I guess I need a lawyer."

He didn't say another word as they read him his rights and led him out.

Epilogue

"So you finally got him, but only after wasting all that time because you blinded yourself to the solution – twice," Dave said. "How did the crab traps do? I designed the trapdoor type. This was a test of them."

"They caught about the same number of blue crabs as the big traps, plus a lot of stone crabs," Alma said. "They take up a lot less room. They're easier to use."

"That's some picture of Mike," he said, looking at it hanging on the wall.

"It's very good, don't you think?" Alma asked.

"It's much better than good, it's art. I suppose Mike spends all his time here blushing, now. What does Annette say about it?"

"She says it's beautiful," I said. "Mac McMullins wants you to help him try to stop them from ruining the area south of Coconut Road."

"There's no way in hell to save that stretch! I've been all over the damned world and I've never seen anything as corrupt and just plain stupid as this place. Anything any big developer wants, he gets. It's foregone. It's the way of things here and it'll stay the way of things here. I'm tired of wasting my time fighting for these idiot asses. They want to leave a legacy like they're building for their kids around here, fine. The human race is on the way out. The sooner, the better. I just hope something better comes along to replace us. I hope we don't make the world unlivable for everything while we destroy ourselves with our innate stupidity."

Yep! Dave and Mac will get along fine!

Don't Push

Prologue

It was an exceptional kind of day. There was a light breeze coming in off the gulf from the southwest, raising a slight chop on the bay that cooled the air nicely – though I never minded the heat in Englewood.

Alma was putting the orchid plants back in place in the medium house. I'd just put the awards and trophies in their case and was waiting for Jim Barrow, my boatman, to come back in with Cal Jones and his wife, Wilma. Paulo, my groundskeeper, came to sit with me to discuss planting a larger vegetable garden. It was the first of February and things should be planted right away.

His wife, Louisa, had their kid, Cal and Wilma's one, and my three on the terrace, telling them a story – in Spanish.

Those kids aren't really sure who their real parents are anymore – none of them!

We decided to plant more okra, tomatoes, onions, green peas, snap beans and corn, and to keep the rest just about the way it was the past year. The collards would last all year here and the mustard would soon seed. We had plenty of the greens frozen for the summer.

Len Stewart, county sheriff (homicide) and close friend, drove up to talk a few minutes about a case I handled in Bonita Springs last month and the testimony I'd give. He left when Jim and Cal arrived, after promising to come to a fresh fish and hushpuppy dinner that night with his ladyfriend. Cal and Wilma would be there, as would Mike Nelson, half-owner of the private airport in Sarasota where

I keep my jet, his steady girlfriend, Annette, Tony Jacobi, general genius at the Crane plant I own in Sarasota and his wife, the former Shirley Bock, half-owner of the airport – and maybe Dave, a friend who writes those "Maita" SF books.

Cal, Jim and I got in the Stamas and headed out toward Stump Pass out of Lemon Bay to try to get some fresh pompano for dinner. The water inland was cloudy, showing someone was illegally dredging somewhere.

"Want to find where it's coming from?" Jim asked.

"No. I really don't give a damn anymore."

"Been talking to Dave again?" Cal asked. "You sound like he does, lately."

Cal doesn't much care for Dave. There's some kind of weird chemical irritation between them (Like the one between Slats Lattimore, coroner, and me), but, lately, Dave's helping Cal write a book or something, so it's not as bad as it used to be. Cal was finding that writing wasn't nearly as easy as his job with FHP.

"I was just reading about a big developer who wants a special tax district for a subdivision at Bonita. The district will impact on a hell of a lot of people who have nothing to do with that development. They also want a special ruling that could allow them to annex a trailer park in the area. They could then condemn those peoples' property and throw them out."

"What are you griping about?" Jim asked. "Hell, they'd never be allowed to do anything like that!"

"Hell, I'll bet you they *will* be allowed to do *exactly* that!" I shot back. "Any bigshit developer can do anything he wants down there now, and it's getting that way, here.

"There's a county commissioner who met with a group

opposed to the district because they don't have water, sewers, roads or even electricity for the place. He's close personal friends with a bigshot engineer who works for the developer. He stood in front of those people and assured them all the problems were solved and there wouldn't be any problems whatever. The people were taken in by the cheap little tinhorn and agreed not to fight it.

"I live down there about half the time. They're going to build a couple thousand houses in that place where there are no problems with anything – and they've put us on water restrictions and are already talking about making them stronger. The electric company sent out a flyer in the bills that says we might have brownouts if there's any severe weather this summer because they don't have the capacity to supply increases for what's already *there*!

"There's no water and no electricity for what's there now, but there won't be any problem with adding a few thousand more people to the system?

"There's a very slight tiny little problem with the fact the roads won't carry the traffic in any emergency where evacuation is called for – so they're going to add a few thousand homes and eight or ten highrises.

"Of course *taxes* will have to be raised on everybody so the local politicians can pay ridiculous salaries to their friends in consultant firms – and the Fort Myers papers had several whole sections of lists of people who were about to lose their property because they couldn't pay the taxes *now*!

"Oh, sure! They won't allow anything like *that*!

"Like *hell* they won't! It's just a matter of having the right friend in politics. That sleazeball bunch of slime doesn't care about anything but their own pockets."

"Vote them out," Cal suggested. "You have enough to run campaigns for anyone you want."

"They already did that. They elected a new commissioner who has the critical vote on a multimillion dollar project – who's sleeping with a married person who works for the same company the deal's to be with. Great quality we have there. There's no undue influence on the vote. What's the big fuss? The sordid affair can be broken off until after the vote, so it'll be hunky-dory! No influence if they aren't sleeping together at the precise moment the vote's taken!

"If I found anyone with one tenth that much influence acting in half as blatant a manner in Crane they'd be bounced so fast they wouldn't know what hit them! I'd add a complete criminal investigation of them to it and try to have their asses in the pen for the next five to fifteen!"

"You *do* sound like Dave! Why not do like he says and move out of the country?"

"He's going down through the Caribbean and along the Mexican Gulf Coast to try to find a place. If he can find something really good, I'll very probably do exactly that. I'd move back to Nicely, but I swore I'd never go back to cold winters again, and I damned well meant it. I was thinking about moving to Australia, but they have their own problems with corruption."

"You're serious, aren't you?"

"Serious as cancer."

"If you sell out this place and the Bonita place, won't you be giving in to the bunch of slimy crooks doing those things?" Jim asked. "I mean, they want your land so bad they can taste it!"

"I'll put the land in secure trust with Crane for wildlife preserves like I did with that Everglades property."

"Why not donate it to the state and save the taxes?" Cal asked with a grin (he knows the last thing I care about is taxes).

"Because the state would redefine its use and sell it to the developers. I can afford the taxes. They're all the same kinds of crooks. It's the new American way.

"The thing that started me thinking this way is how the water shortage is being handled around here. I think it should serve to show people exactly whose interests are being protected, and by whom.

"There's a water management district whose board members are selected through state political appointment. It consists mainly of builders and developers, so the homeowners and renters are under those tighter restrictions, while development and building goes on at the same pace. The fact that the board represents a blatant conflict of interest, in itself, doesn't count for anything.

"When Dave was writing those editorials about things, he was very popular with the editors of the papers in the area. When he started pointing out the local little-tin-god type politician wasn't doing what he was saying, they stopped printing his stuff. I always thought the press had a certain basic responsibility, but the papers down there seem to be the first ones to kiss up to the big developers and corrupt big frogs."

"But you're not really serious about moving out, are you?" Cal asked. "You're our closest friends!"

"I can't stay around a population of people who are willfully stupid. I really don't know if I'm serious or not. I think it'll take very little to make me go. I will say that."

We changed the subject then to more pleasant things.

We managed to catch three large pompano for dinner,

then headed back in. When we got back in and cleaned the fish we sat around talking about whatever came up until the rest of our guests came, then had a delicious meal before going out into the screened area by the entrance to the greenhouses for coffee and cognac. We talked until after midnight, then the guests went home and those of us at the house went to bed.

It was a quarter after five in the morning when Mac McMullins, a friend and neighbor at the Bonita Springs place, called to say Lorna and her husband had found a dead body while pulling their gill nets near the mouth of the Imperial River in the bay. "Sean figured you'd be interested in this one. The guy has a bullet hole right between the eyes. Lorna called me on the CB and said to tell you to get your ass down here."

I said I'd be down in about an hour. Alma woke up and asked if I had a case and I said I did. She's used to that. She sighed and went back to sleep.

Chapter one

The trip to Bonita Springs on I-75 doesn't take long, now that they've completed the repairs, and I'm a special marshal for the state grand jury, so can use an E-light on the car (and siren, but didn't need that) if I'm involved in an investigation. This case didn't really apply, but Len and the FHP let me get by – to a point. If there had been much traffic they would ream me a new one for it, probably.

I went directly through the trailer village and to the McMullins' place on their canal, where Lorna and Mac came out to meet me.

Mac is Sean's father. Sean is Lorna's husband. The part of the family living in Florida (they're originally from Tennessee) are commercial fishermen. Mac is something of an activist. He's the area character in several ways. He and Dave, who we were discussing yesterday afternoon, often work together on some of the local environmental projects, which is neither here nor there. Just information.

"Sean's still out there with the Marine Patrol," Mac said. "I've got to get to the fish wholesalers with this stuff Lorna brought in, so I'll leave you in her hands."

We waved at each other and he got in his truck and drove off.

"What's it all about?" I asked Lorna. "Tell me exactly what happened first and your suspicions or whatever later, when I have some basis."

"We saw a good run of mullet in close to the mangroves by the shell islands out in the bay from the river. It isn't by the main river, it's by that creek runnel that comes off to the north, but you can go through down to the river, if you know how. There's a pretty strong current through there. Tidal.

"We dropped a drag anchor by the reeds – do you know anything about that part of the river mouth?"

"Not very much."

"Well, it sort of snakes around out there. Salt marsh reeds come out and mix with the mangroves. Some places, it's hard to tell, except at high or low tides, because there are so many little reed islands and oyster shoals. It's more like a swamp than the bay, but high tide, you can go all around and low, you can see the channels, because there's nothing else with water.

"We struck our nets and circled around past a lot of the side runnels, so we don't know which one he washed out of, but we're sure he came from the main river run somewhere because there isn't anywhere else out there for him to have gotten in the water we could see. We think he was probably dumped from the bridge on forty one and washed out with the tide. It's been coming in since about six. It was still going out when we found him.

"We called Mac on the CB and he called the Marine Patrol, then he went out and brought me and the fish in. Sean's waiting there until Johnny shows up.

"Johnny's the Marine Patrolman. It took him almost 'til now to get in because it's so shallow at low tide. The patrol boat's too deep a draft to come in under power, so he had to pole it. Sean's waiting to try to help Johnny figure when and where he was probably dumped. They're figuring the tide and water speeds and the distance and all that.

"I told Mac to call you and waited until Johnny came across the flats about twenty minutes ago. He took one look and said he could figure it pretty easy, then I went back to wait for you at the house. Johnny says he's sure it's just another of those drug deals gone sour and we're wasting the taxpayers' money even fooling with it. He's sure he's seen the guy out in the gulf with some known dealers a couple of times when he was out checking incoming party boats.

"I think he'd rather mark it up to that and forget it. He really gets off on those drug dealers, sometimes. He's funny that way. He rants it's nothing but a waste to do anything at all, so long as all they're doing is killing each other off. It saves money to look the other way."

"The coroner can figure time of death a hell of a lot better than we can. Modern techniques can give time of death to within a few minutes, in most cases. The important things are what kind of gun was used and from what distance and angle and whether he was standing, sitting, prone or whatever."

"They're trying to figure when he was dumped off the bridge, not when he was shot. It's not impossible someone saw the car there."

I said I'd run on out to my place and get the small boat out, but Lorna said she'd take me out in the net boat. It was channeled and didn't draw much water.

The tide still wasn't in much, so we boarded and headed out into the bay. The net boat will travel in eight inches of water, so we were able to cut across the flats, which I couldn't do in my boat because it drew 11 inches of water, minimum, and that at idle speed. I'd have to pole along in close, which would take a lot of time.

Lorna stayed over the sand. She wouldn't cut the grass up with the motor. Mac had ranted too often about the fact those idiots who did that were ruining the very spots the fish they depended on for their living bred!

We were at the scene in only seven minutes. The Marine Patrol boat was tied to Sean's net boat and the Sheriff's boat was to one side. They'd had to maneuver both of those boats in with the poles, so hadn't nearly finished the job there. The coroner had the body in a bag and was discussing something with Lt. Sam Lukens, the detective in charge of homicide for the county. Sam waved to me and had the coroner show me the body. He first introduced me to Johnny, then I took a look at the body.

The bullet, a large caliber high-impact load, had entered just above the right eye and had taken the entire back of the head away when it exited. He hadn't been dead for long.

"Know who he was?"

"Not a clue, yet," Sam replied. "I won't call it a drug crime – but it's probably a drug crime. It's like the pattern for this sort of thing. Sean and Johnny figure the tide took about an hour and a half to bring him this far."

"Exactly where was the body, Sean?"

"As near as I can figure, over where the red balloon's tied to the reeds. The net might have rolled him twenty feet or so this way. We were striking from up and around and back this way."

"Is there any chance he was around to the other side of the island?"

"No. He was on this side and not more than twenty feet from the balloon. Why?"

"The tide's flowing in and spilling around the island by the oysters on this side. That means he was deposited there on the incoming tide or he'd be on the other side."

"There's a swirl right there that would roll him along and

back around to there, see? Anyone who knows water knows how all that works. The tide swirls to the lee side."

"That loose flannel shirt would catch on the oysters and swing him in over to the end of the island. The oysters run off both ends. That's what forms these things. If a swirl put him there it had to be from the side it's flowing now. The tide's coming IN, at the moment.

"If he was dropped off the bridge it was an hour and a half or more before low tide last night, which would make it at about eight thirty at the latest – so he wasn't dropped off the bridge. The traffic's far too heavy that time of the night."

"You really are good!" Lorna exclaimed. "Why don't we run up this side runnel to the river and on up a ways and see if maybe there's another spot where he could've been dumped in?"

Johnny shook his head and Sean grinned. Sam saluted and turned back to the coroner.

Lorna started the motor and we cruised slowly up the runnel. There was nothing for quite a distance other than the mangroves, oysters, driftwood and reeds, then the river. On the river, we stayed to the south bank and approached a couple of developments. I studied the banks as we cruised along slowly, but he could have been dropped off any of the properties along the river.

We went up to the bridge, then headed back along the north side of the river, which was much the same. Lorna waved at others as we passed and headed out into the bay. She suggested I might like to see what was along the path the current followed on the incoming tide.

Mac was just then coming in in his boat and we waved at him. There were two other commercial net boats sitting off a short distance, watching. Lorna waved at one of them and ignored the other, telling me he was one of the assholes who made it so hard on the whole group of mullet fishermen by insisting on treating the local landowners and private fishermen like nothing more than an obstacle to his business. She said only a few of them have that attitude, but all of them paid for it. It was one of Mac's causes. Some people seemed to think the fact that *they* had rights meant nobody else did.

"We had a light breeze from the northeast all night so it didn't push the body around much," Lorna said when we were on the bay. "He could have been killed anywhere along here or in the sweep up that way. The only stronger flow would come from the south along by those two oyster shoals or in a ways from those two little islands out there. The flow splits on them from the pass.

"The channel to the north end of the bay goes up that side and to here and comes in sort of in a wide sweep out there to the oyster shoals. The run to the river goes between them and the main flow to Bonita goes out there in the waterway through Intrepid."

"It doesn't go on in and flow south along the shoreline?"

"Spring Creek comes in a little south of the islands and has a strong outflow for a long time after the tide changes. The flow from that pushes the tidal flow out. That's what formed the oyster beds where they are. Silt and stuff drops where the flows meet, a bit of wood sticks in it, barnacles grow on the wood, oysters grow on the barnacles, they catch more crap, and it builds. After a few years there's a solid limestone base from the old oysters and the shoals spread out and soon stabilize the flow channels. Another five years and mangroves will start growing on the oysters and we'll have another cap island. There's a mangrove already growing on that little inner shoal in there. Another one will start forming out that way and the islands will march right on out.

"Don't look at me like that. Mac studies that kind of thing for his causes and I sort of absorb some of it."

I grinned and said, "Go along the south flow for as far as he might've washed in about three hours. That's about as long as it could've been. He wouldn't have moved fast, rolling along the bottom."

"He had a plastic raincoat on when we found him. I guess the sheriff took it off to examine the body, but there was some air in a sort of bubble holding him a few inches under the surface. He could have washed a long way on the tide. I'll make it three hours with that in the equation."

I nodded and we headed along the path. It was possible the raincoat would've prevented his being entangled on the oysters and he might have been pushed around the reed island by a swirl. I mentioned that to Lorna, who said the raincoat was in a wad floating above him and the flannel shirt was hanging open, so it wasn't likely – both Sam and Johnny would have jumped right on that fact, otherwise.

We went around to the west and came back into the runnel from the direction of the pass, but there wasn't anything obvious to see.

Sam was just heading out, led by the Marine Patrol boat. We waved as we passed them and went on to tell Mac and Sean we'd meet them at my house for breakfast, then Lorna headed back.

There weren't any runnels or rivers before Spring Creek, then the bays from Coconut Road, but he could have been dumped there on the early part of the outgoing tide and would wash along the southern drift route and back in when the tide changed. I asked Lorna to head in at Coconut Road and we went close to the fish camp there and on in as far as there would have been sufficient current to carry a body out, then back to meet Mac and Sean, who were passing. We went on to my place and talked a bit over breakfast. I said I thought the body came from around the Coconut Road runnel. I would know when we had a time of death established. If it was too short a time, he was dumped in the bay or from a piece of real estate along the river.

I went to the McMullins' place with Lorna to get my car. All I could do was wait, so I worked on the orchids until noon, then went to see Sam.

"Bill figures the time of death at about ten o'clock last night," Sam said. "It was probably done with a three fifty seven. Magnum load. Did a lot of damage.

"He might be a guy name of Edward S. Zimmer. Everything fits. We don't have prints or anything, but his car was found in the center median on forty one between Coconut Road and Corkscrew. We're lifting prints from the car to try to match. Dan Ford's on that. If that's Ed Zimmer he was thirty two years old and was a construction worker with a subcontractor working on the development north of where he was found.

"The reason we're working on that so much is because we tried to reach him about his car and his landlady said he didn't come home last night. We checked the job. He didn't show up for work today. The general description fits, but we haven't had anyone in to identify the body. Zimmer doesn't have any local relatives. Dan's going to try to get the foreman to identify. The landlady refuses."

"Anything at all on him?"

"Dan's gathering the stuff. I'll have to wait for something to go on. He doesn't have a record and the foreman says he's dependable. Landlady says the rent's always paid in advance. That's all I have, so far."

We talked a bit longer, then I considered where the car was found and what I already thought and headed for Coconut Road, where I checked the entire area near the water, then went to the fish camp where some of the local fishermen hang out. I mentioned being friends with Lorna, Sean and Mac, and asked them about the place and about Coconut Road.

There are always a few cars along the side of the canal in the evening and fairly often at night, so no one paid any attention to them. Some drunks come along now and then and have to be run off when they get loud. There was a little noise the past night at around nine thirty, but they quietened down. They'd been popping off firecrackers. Gus Barton probably went over and told them to get the hell out or he'd call the cops. He was closest to the place and usually handled that kind of stuff.

I drove over to the Barton place, but Gus said he'd been in Naples the past night at a party with his girlfriend and didn't get in until well past midnight.

Next stop was back to the canal at the point closest to the Barton place to have a closer look, where I found what appeared to be some bloodstains. I used the CB in the Jeep to call Dan, who came right over with the lab van and the crew. They made a minute search of the area, finding a dime and a pocket comb to go along with the bloodstains. I told about the noise and about Gus not being home. Dan went to the fish camp to talk to the bunch there. There wasn't anything else I could do, so I drove on back home, got my little bay boat, and went by water to where the lab crew was finishing up. They said they found a little penknife and some hair and blood on the rock fill a few inches above the high water line.

Dan got in my boat and we headed very slowly out, searching among the mangrove roots at the water's edge for anything that might have gotten tangled there.

"The tide changed at ten forty two. I read the chart at the fish camp. It had almost three hours to carry the body outward. The tide's very slow in that canal, so he'd take more than half an hour to move the little distance out to the channel."

"The tide's almost full now. The meander would carry the body across and out by those mangroves." He pointed to a long bank of the thick plants to our left. We checked the mangroves, but found nothing. We followed the tide stream out along the channel to where we thought the body might have been at low tide.

"He was between here and that marker in there," Dan deduced. "There're shallow flats to either side, so he would wash back in along the same channel when the tide changed and would end up at the fish camp or in that little bay north of it. This isn't working!"

"If he was about a hundred feet back toward the fish camp the swirl from the changing tidals would push him off toward that island."

We moved slowly toward the oyster/mangrove island, where my depth finder showed a small channel running directly toward the inward side of the island.

"It's the flow channel to Spring Creek! He'd wash right

in there!"

"The breeze was from northeast about twelve to fifteen knots, which would push him along behind the island in there or would push him back outward again between the islands if there were no current to move him on south. Lorna said the flow to Spring Creek is weak until you're close."

"She'd know. Those fishermen know about every little current in the bay under any conditions. The problem I see is that the breeze wouldn't affect him. He wasn't above the water, at all."

"The breeze moves the surface of the water itself, a little. The current's strong toward the south after you pass that island at low tides because there's so little feed to the bay. I've done a study on the flushing the bay gets, and it ain't much in the little coves and canals. There simply isn't anywhere for that volume of water to come in. It's only three or four inches deep on those flats at low tide this time of year, so the flow's heavier in those cross-channels. The flow stays pretty much only in those channels until it's over those flats to the south. Once the body was past this island, the run from Spring Creek keeps coming out for a good hour after the tide changes at the New Pass bridge, so the incoming tide along here would meet the flow from the creek about where that southernmost marker is and would push the body on south."

We watched the depth finder and, sure enough, there was a narrow secondary flow channel southward and slightly outward at the last marker to the south.

"From here on it's pretty much like Lorna said. We came along to the inside of those oyster shoals – well, there were shoals at low tide."

"Then there were shoals when the body came by. If it wasn't pretty much at dead low tide and incoming the body wouldn't have come this way at all."

We went to the shoals, which were a few inches under water at high tide. I took out the glassbottomed viewer I carry to look for scallops (Except there are no scallops in Estero Bay) and moved very slowly around the outer sand shoal.

Nothing.

We moved to the inner shoal and repeated the process, finding a small triangle of smoky plastic on the oysters.

"It's the same kind of stuff his raincoat was made out of. If there's a tear in it that matches this I owe you a drink! That would be some kind of deducing!"

"Elementary, my dear Watson!" I intoned. "If one will only consider with the little gray cells the problem and apply oneself with diligence to the puzzle presented by the events piling up on the shores of the mind one will confuse oneself so much one will have no idea what one was about to say.

"The body would move from here in a slow wide arc toward the runnels where they found it. It's all sand bottom between here and there, so we have the whole thing solved as to how the body got there and where it came from – if we establish it to that shoal. Hopefully, that little scrap of plastic will do that for us. I think we can count on the bloodstains and hair proving he was killed at Coconut Road. We won't find anything more between here and the runnel where he was found because the bottom's smooth and unobstructed, so let's head in. I'll get the Jeep and take you back to your car and you can fill me in on anything else you've found, if you will."

It was definitely Edward Zimmer. They got a picture at his rental unit and a receipt from a doctor who treated him for a broken finger four months ago. The finger on the body was the one the doctor set. No one knew any reason anyone would kill him. He very definitely wasn't involved in any drug deals. Most people liked him and others were neutral, at worst.

"Sam and I were going to go over to his rental when you called about the blood and noise," Dan said. "I'll call Sam on your CB and we can meet him there. Maybe we'll find some clues, but I doubt it. This may be some crazies or druggies. We get more of them every year. They seem to go on violence sprees for no reason, whatever. I guess that's part of the area's rapid growth and is something we have to expect and live with."

"Yeah. It's societal. Drugs, dropout students, violence without reason and the rest of it are all part of the failure of politics. It's all a part of the great greed that seems to be growing faster than the population. Greed and frustration don't mix! Dave keeps harping about it, and I'm beginning to agree."

"Dave? You mean your author friend? I read all those letters to the editors he writes. I never quite get the connection. He leaves something out to where it doesn't make any sense. He mostly seems to rant."

"They very carefully edit – read modify – what he writes, and leave out the included explanations. I was with him once when he was talking on the phone with a reporter about a developer. He said `It's not that I'm against any development at all. I merely think sewers and water should be in place before any construction begins.' She quoted him as saying `It's not *only* that I'm against any development....' You can see how adding one little word changes it a hundred eighty degrees.

"Say you're graduating from high school tomorrow. Tell me what you're going to be?"

"I don't expect I'll start off as first vice president of the company, if that's what you mean."

"You think it's enough these young kids today know they might actually become *manager* of a McDonald's or Burger King? Can you show me where they can realistically look for anything better than that?"

"A certain number will make it! There were *never* any guarantees!"

"How many? What percent? What percent have a real shot at ever being anything?"

"I guess, very few. I see what you mean. I have no idea what to do about it."

"It mostly comes back to what we call a service-based economy. American investors got too lazy. Taking chances with a new idea is now out. You have to be conservative with your funds. Progress stops, and anyone who WILL take a chance will become a dominant force in international power politics when something eventually pays off, then the conservatives become buyers instead of sellers. This country doesn't produce anything anymore – not anything anyone else is interested in buying. We've lost the edge we've always had. Innovation doesn't come from here anymore and our government won't stand up for it's own people."

"If you have any answers, I'm willing to listen."

"I have a couple. They're based on logic, not on what some panel of experts – who got us in this mess in the first place – comes up with. The powers that be have it too easy being able to vote themselves all kinds of perks and raises, so they aren't about to listen.

"We have a murder case. I'll let Dave write his little letters to the editors to try to get through to the people, but it won't work with a population who don't want to hear it."

Dan called Sam to meet us at the victim's rental unit and we headed out and down toward Alico Road.

The cabin was a bit back in a wooded section that wasn't so overdeveloped as most of the area and wasn't bad, at all. There were ten individual cabins behind the large old house where the landlady lived. They were all alike, consisting of a living room with kitchenette on the back end, a bedroom and a bath. The unit Zimmer had lived in was comfortable, clean, and efficient, if not expensive.

The landlady said a maid came in to vacuum and dust, change the sheets, towels, bedclothes, and so forth, but it's up to the individual to take care of their own dishes and personal laundry, though a couple of them, Zimmer included, paid the maid to do their laundry for them. Each cabin paid its own electrical bills, but gas was supplied for heating and cooking with the rent. There was a carport beside the unit with a steel shed with a padlock at the back.

"Each one's gotta keep the grass cut fer his own unit," Mrs. Kissle, the landlady, said. "Part of the deal. Cita's husband, Juan, cuts it fer most of 'em. Charges five bucks each'n cuts it ever two weeks. They ain't much'a it, so's it's a good deal fer everbody all around.

"I don't know why anyone'd want to kill Ed. He were all right, fer a Jew. Real generous'n helped all'n us if'n we asked. Fixed Juan's mower fer 'im and didn't even charge nothin' fer labor."

"It seems only the good ones get killed anymore," Dan agreed. "Scum gets away with anything. Courts are all for the crook and good honest people get the royal shaft!"

Sam and I strolled off while Dan became fast friends with Mrs. Kissle. If there was anything to be learned from her, he'd learn it. Sam said he was raised right around that area and what he was saying, he believed. Sam couldn't disagree, because there had been another murder recently by a violent criminal a judge had let out of the lockup on a low bond, despite the cries from the police and prosecutors about him being a professional violent criminal who wouldn't change and wasn't even a little rehabilitable.

We used the passkey to get into unit four. Zimmer had been a very neat person, it seemed. The bed was made up by the maid, but there weren't any clothes laying around. All the magazines were in a stack. There weren't any dirty dishes, and the place was a lot cleaner than merely a basic vacuuming.

We started in the kitchen, finding nothing out of the ordinary there. The living room had a TV and a VCR. There were several rented movies, all recent hits. No X-rated or such crap. The magazines were mostly "Omni" and "National Geographic" and so forth. There were five or six videotapes in a drawer in an end table by a sofa, so I put one in the VCR and let it play while we looked around. It was a home video of what was, apparently, a fishing trip with a few friends. Ed Zimmer was in only a few shots, twice with an arm around an attractive dark girl he called Cindy. Sam read the counter and wrote a note.

We dropped in the rest of the home videos and watched a scene here and there. Sam said he'd turn them over to the lab to have everyone in them identified, but he didn't expect much.

The bedroom didn't give us anything except a strongbox in a closet with the title to his car, automobile and health insurance papers, old IRS forms, and that sort of thing. The video camera was behind the box, but there was no tape in it.

We found it in the bathroom in a little leather shaving kit wrapped in a handkerchief. As soon as I saw it I said, "That's got to be something important!" at the same time as Dan, who had joined us, said the same thing.

Sam took the tape and put it in the VCR while Dan and I sat on the sofa to watch. It didn't make any sense to me. There were shots of several cars stopping at a partially finished house, people going in and coming out and longrange views of four men talking at the construction site where Zimmer was working. Dan said he recognized the building shown in certain views and the cars parked out behind the subjects.

"Do you recognize any of the people?" Sam asked.

"That guy in the blue flannel shirt looks sorta familiar," Dan replied.

The tape ran on, panning the cars and the buildings, then the camera suddenly zoomed in on the four, who seemed to be arguing. The sound didn't come through at the distance, so we weren't sure of that, but Dan and Sam both exclaimed at the same time at the closeup, saying "Reynolds!"

"Who's Reynolds?" I asked.

"A very wealthy development financier, local, who seems to be too connected with some rather unsavory characters," Sam said. "Unless those others are supposed to be someone special, I don't get it!"

"It all depends on what's in that!" I said, as Reynolds handed another of the men a briefcase. The man opened the case, looked in, snapped it shut, and nodded. They all shook hands and turned to go. One of them suddenly looked over, yelled something and pointed at the camera. The tape ended.

"So! They didn't get him then or we wouldn't have the tape," Sam deduced. "We can assume they didn't get him for a day or two. I can find very closely when the tape was made."

"The truss company truck on the road?"

"Yes. Those are trusses for the building Dan recognized being built, so we can find when they were delivered.

"You're positive about the building, Dan? They have six or eight models, so they pretty much look alike."

"That thirty four in black letters on the block work and the two pine trees with that portable toilet under them and that sick coconut palm," Dan answered. "The trusses are still only about a third up, or that was true when I was there this morning to check on a tip about a drug deal and a local bigwig."

"Then the videotape was made yesterday. They get the trusses in place pretty fast."

"Then this little tape has to be damned important!" Sam exclaimed.

"Let's get to the office and get some ID on the rest of these people," Dan suggested. "I think this tape has to be what we're looking for. The lab crew can finish up here."

We reached the office, where the captain tried to get me out. He said no private snoop was going to interfere in any of his investigations, millionaire or not. I showed him the official ID papers denoting me as a registered state expert investigator for the courts and the ones naming me a special marshal for the grand jury. I've done a lot of work for the state, and both positions are salaried. I get a dollar for each appearance I make in court and am allowed to sit at the prosecutor's table in any trial I'm involved in. I also have a special authorization to question witnesses, in certain rare instances.

He glared, but let me go in with Sam and Dan.

It took almost two hours to identify the first one we were looking for. His name was Antonio (Tony Money) Roberto Moreni, an affiliated member of the Farris gang from Detroit. They were into unions, protection, insurance, drugs, fencing, prostitution, and anything else that came along. They were known to be trying to get into the cruise business in Florida because they could run casinos on the ships as soon as they were past the limits.

"It looks like we've stumbled onto something a lot bigger than I want to work on!" Dan cried. "Damn! Organized crime should only be on the tube!"

"That could cost Reynolds everything," Sam agreed. "We have two people with very definite motives who might have used some syndicate muscle or hit man to get rid of their problem. We have to know who those other two are."

"I'm sure I've seen that blond guy around," Dan said. "I *know* I've seen him somewhere – and a lot more than once. There's some reason I've seen him somewhere.... I've got it! He's a regular deliveryman or something like that. I've seen him on patrol."

"Then why would he even be in this kind of mess? A financier and a hood ... and a truck driver? No way!"

"It all has to do with the construction industry," Sam

suggested. "Maybe he's a truck driver who hijacks building materials by the truckload?

"I can get theft to give me readouts about whatever's missing in this end of the state, but I'm sure we'd know about anything major already. We're not talking about any little pickup load of sheetrock with those two involved."

"I have an idea. Let's get a reporter to look at photos the lab pulls from the tape and see what he comes up with. Reporters might have insights into some of this from angles we wouldn't ever consider. They usually know pretty much what anyone in the area who might make the news looks like."

"I can do a hell of a lot better than that!" Sam said, and went out. He returned in a few minutes with a woman in tow.

"Lydia, CD Grimes," he introduced. "CD, meet Lydia Harper, crime reporter for the local liberal bleeding-heart press."

We shook hands. She asked what we wanted her for, adding that she wasn't about to reveal any of her sources, with or without any stupid court order. She grinned as she said it, so she knew it wasn't anything like that. I didn't say anything.

Dan turned on the tape at the zoom shot. I pointed at it.

"P. P. Reynolds, Ken Pratz, two I don't know. What's the scam?"

"Who's Ken Pratz?" Sam asked.

"Zoning board chief. Is this some crooked deal? I'd dearly love that! I'd like to wrap that Reynolds bastard in something that'd cost him every stinking dirty dollar he ever screwed out of some retired widow with his shoddy houses and TV promos!"

"If you'll guarantee to hold off until we clear up a detail or two, I'll tell you who one of the others in this video happens to be. We'll guarantee you the scoop – and I promise you it'll be national news or better!

"We're investigating a murder, and those four cruds are probably our culprits. We can't let them even guess we have this. It's what the victim died for. If you do anything to warn them and let any one of them get away with this I'll personally see you never work again, anywhere. You know who I am and you know I can do it."

"Deal!" she said with a grin. "I know all about you. I know you back up anything you say and I also know you're straighter than any cop in this state – which ain't saying a whole lot. How's anybody gonna bribe a multibillionaire?

"Give!"

I ran the tape ahead until where the case was being transferred to the unidentified man on the end.

Lydia whistled, and said, "That was as obvious a bribe as I've ever seen! What else do you need? They obviously saw the person taking the video, so they obviously killed him!"

"The video was hidden in the victim's home, meaning there was time between the taking of the video and the crime," Dan cautioned, sternly. "You know how that works. You're the first one to jump in to defend those scum because of something like that. You'd scream reasonable doubt across your headlines and totally ignore any other evidence. You've done it before."

"Don't get into a fight over the press and how vicious and brutal we are to these sweet, gentle types," Sam said, dryly. "I think even Lydia can't defend Reynolds. He's the type she's always against.

"We have a deal. CD damned well means what he said.

"The turkey in the blue shirt is Tony Moreni. Detroit and New York. Ring any bells?"

She whistled again, and nodded.

"So whatever this is, it's also a laundering scheme for the Farris Franchise?"

"Looks that way. Now we have to find out who the fourth man is."

Lydia grabbed the phone on the desk and dialed, asked for Lou, said there was something too big for one person and he'd kick himself for the rest of his life if he didn't get his ass there five minutes ago.

"I called Lou Prinz. He's the home section and keeps an eye on the types like Reynolds and Pratz. He broke that deal where a certain huge conglomerate whose name, RIINT, I won't mention, was using all that reject tile roofing from Michigan on all those expensive houses. If anyone in this county can identify people in the development ripoffs, he can. If it has anything at all to do with construction – or anything else on a house, road, ditch, sewer – he *knows*!"

We chatted a few minutes until a very proper elderly man came in. Lydia pointed at the picture on the screen before anyone said a word and I brought up the zoom shots.

"P. P. Reynolds, Ken Pratz, and Tate DuMont talking with what looks like a cheap hood," he identified, quickly.

"Syndicate. Farris Franchise. Motown," Lydia replied. Prinz whistled louder and longer than Lydia had.

"We'll need background," Lydia continued. "This is big enough to share bylines on.

"Who's Tate DuMont?"

"Supervisor of building inspections, new construction.

Known for handling the really big ones, personally. You know what that means in this county, but we can't prove one single thing. He's sharp, and he'll fool you. Good actor.

"Reynolds is financing several of the bigger local land ripoff projects. We're talking over a billion in the next ten years on two of them. The background on him is public record. They get him cold. Not just a smoking gun, they watch him fire the shot. The evidence disappears and witnesses who were absolutely sure of their facts suddenly get amnesia or say they made it up, then retire to the Bahamas or Mexico or something with a lot of money in the bank they couldn't explain if they were still here.

"Ken Pratz is a wimpy type who DuMont controls, completely. He follows him arou...!" The tape was to the part where the case was exchanged. Prinz turned over his chair as he jumped up, yelling, "You *got* the dirty stinking son of a bitch! You got him *cold*! This time he takes the goddamned fall! You got the rotten bastard handing a bribe right flat to that thug...!

"Where's a phone I can use?! That one?"

"We have to wait with it," Lydia said. "They hope to tag the whole bunch of them for murder one – which is a hell of a lot better than bribery. We've waited a long time for the big one. It's here. We get an exclusive. Guaranteed. Grimes will chew us both up and spit us out in little bloody pieces if we screw it up. He'll damned well do it!

"We've got a rock-solid guarantee, Lou. From Grimes, not the stupid crooked cops. He doesn't play games."

Dan and Sam grinned. I saw this was just a game they played and that they really did respect one another. Sam didn't go out and bring her in because he hated her guts.

We discussed the case a bit. We gave them everything we

had (within reason) and they gave us all the gossip and facts about the four in the tape. They would write it up with a special code on the computers and have it ready as soon as we gave them the go-ahead with it. They'd wait a reasonable time, but not months.

Now was the time to find the actual killer or killers so we could tie them securely to those four lovely people or some combination within that select little group.

Dan picked up a list from his desk, read it over and said, "Hmm! That little plastic bit you found in the bay *did* come from his raincoat! I owe you a drink."

Chapter two

"It's up to you," Sam said. "Dan and I have to get back to the case from the angle of the department, which says we go after those four and try to break them down. It's a good thing Captain Knowland doesn't know what we have or we'd have orders to handle this like we don't want to. We can give our reports, saying we're following several leads, but don't have anything definite. Knowland's by the book, so we'd end up letting them know we had something, if he catches on, which would give them incentive to cover their asses and we'd lose them in the long run, anyhow.

"Maybe you'd better handle it like you did that Bonnie Bond case and only have us there when you sew it up – ha! Ha!

"We'll follow what we have. I'll get the dope on Moreni and the Farris bunch and run down whatever I can on Reynolds. They're from out of town, so we have the edge on that part of it.

"You work on DuMont and Pratz, OK?"

"Suits me. I'll start with them and see where it goes. I can pretend Crane's looking for a place to build some kind of top secret facility for one of the government's little projects and want to know about the local zoning and construction laws – and how to get around them. It can be one of those things with toxic wastes or materials we have to store or seal, so we'll definitely have to meet with the inspection teams to be sure we can afford to put such a big and expensive plant in this county where they can rake something off."

"Make it something that would be easiest to handle with

some under-the-table payoffs and something you have to get moving on right now," Lydia suggested. "They'll come up with an offer to 'expedite' the permits or something that you can use to break them down. They'll testify against Reynolds to save their own tail feathers."

"That's the basic idea."

"You're purely disgusting!" Lou protested, all big-eyed innocence. "I most certainly would never place myself in the untenable position of suggesting any such thing! Why, it almost *smacks* of entrapment! It's so – so – just dis*gust*ing!

"I hope you understand, we don't want to ever *hear* about any such tactics being used! Come, Lydia, my dear. It's time they made their plans and we certainly aren't authorized to *hear* or know about what they're doing – and we can't very well be against anything we don't *hear* or know about, now can we?

"I wonder if perhaps that stretch of swampy land out by the interstate where nobody could see or know what Crane was doing is still for sale so cheap? Why, if some company were to install leaky, substandard containment vats for toxic wastes it would be *decades* before it would ever leak into the water supply or anything. It's so isolated no one would know what was going on way out there! Some unscrupulous company might even proceed under the assumption that *they* wouldn't be here if anything went wrong! Isn't that a scary idea?"

"Are you talking about the Overton Tract, one mile east of the interstate on the southern end of the county, around six or seven miles north of the county line off Thorntree Road?" Lydia asked. "Yes! It would be just too *horrible* if some unethical company were to use that land in any such horrible way! The idea really *scares* me! Why, no one could know about it for *years*!"

"If some such company came in I'll wager they'd try to find some way to get around making those terribly expensive holding vats, don't you?" I wondered, aloud. "I'm certainly glad we have such honest and forthright inspectors for that kind of thing. As you say, IF there were any dishonest inspectors they could be sure they'd go undetected for decades out there.

"The Overton Tract, you say?"

"Well, Crane Systems has the reputation for not doing anything crooked," Lou said. "At least, if they do anything like that they have the funds to guarantee they'd never get caught at it.

"Isn't it wonderful they don't even have any employees who could offer bribes and that kind of *awful* thing so many of those big corporations do? If they did anything like that in the past I'm sure they were smart enough to have never been caught or I'd have heard about it. You can bet the normal citizen would report to me in minutes if they ever heard about any such travesty!

"Don't you think we should be getting back to the paper, my dear? We *do* have duties we're paid to perform. It's a pity Mr. Grimes is so well-known. If he were to do that kind of thing, personally, they'd know immediately he's the famous detective."

"I guess they would know who I am."

"They don't necessarily know what you look like, John Doe!" Lydia replied. "Particularly if you don't quite look like you."

I pointed a finger at her and made the bang-bang sign with an added wink. She grinned and we all went our own ways. I spent a few minutes considering, grinned and sighed.

Tony Jacobi, my general manager at Crane Systems in Sarasota and husband of Shirley Bock Jacobi, half-owner of the airport where I keep my jet, said he'd get me a portfolio set up from Crane under the name of Stan S. Carr.

"That's Stanley Steamer Carr. You can say that your parents thought it was a great joke or something. No one would believe it was made up."

The important thing now was to figure out some minor kind of disguise to ensure I wouldn't be recognized at the wrong time by someone involved. My picture has been in the papers for too many things and my name was already connected with the case. I didn't need a complicated physical disguise, like the Nigel Blackwaithe thing I've used in some cases, but would use some of the things that one used.

The device behind my teeth to change my voice?

No. They hadn't heard me speak and my voice isn't distinctive to a degree anyone would notice, anyhow. Something so I don't look too much like my slightly blurry newspaper pictures.

I went to the Sarasota plant to let Tony help me. We came up with a wig that looked expensive, but still looked like a wig. That would work on the psychology of the viewer to make him/her picture me as balding. My lush hair would be hidden under the rug and the hairline altered.

Tony's secretary used some makeup from her own pocketbook that made my cheekbones look a lot more prominent and my nose looked sharper. She showed me how to apply the shadows. It didn't take much. Tony took a black-and-white Polaroid shot and we compared the picture from the paper from a case a couple of weeks ago. I really did look like perhaps a relative, but definitely not the same person.

Tony fixed up a company attache' case with all sorts of papers identifying me as land procurer for Crane. There was a "secret" prospectus concerning a plant that would produce unspecified products for the defense department and several memos telling me to "handle" the problem of storage and/or disposal of certain materials. I was to see that the plant was close to a major land transportation route, but was also distanced from any large concentration of population.

Thus armed I headed back homeward.

"I think the parcel east of the interstate is perfect for most of the points in the prospectus," I explained to the woman the county commission board sent to discuss the plant project (Crane actually did want to build a transshipping warehouse in the area and the large tract Lou and Lydia had suggested met or exceeded everything on that project, so I would buy it. The project wasn't to be a total scam). "I'll have to talk with someone who has a complete knowledge of zoning, then I'll have to talk with someone higher up about special types of construction. Also with the code board management and inspection administrators. I'm not interested in talking to a bunch of underlings."

"I can give you the zoning requirements," Miss Relski replied. "It's just part of the growth management files. Comprehensive plans are registered with the state, so that's no problem, anymore."

"This plant will be producing and handling top secret military components for the pentagon! Believe me, Crane has run across a lot of problems that aren't covered in some file, somewhere. I have to have the assurances of the most responsible people in every department we'll be working with before we commit tens of millions of dollars to this kind of major project. I'm not talking about some little neighborhood welding shop here! I do *not* deal with underlings!"

"Tens of millions? Is it really on that scope?"

"We have one hundred nineteen million dollars in the Sarasota plant," I informed her. "You can easily check on that figure – and that's only the permanently attached assets. This project is for a limited term, then we'll convert the plant for something else. We'll probably want to build other types of facilities on the property later. Within ten years this project could become as big as Sarasota, but the nature of the things we produce may change radically in that time-frame. J. R. Crane once made huge computers with thousands of vacuum tubes. They were terribly limited. Now we produce computers with hundreds of chips that are *not* limited!

"In nineteen fifty one, Crane began building a super computer that eventually filled a five story building covering more than a full city block at its base. It could eventually handle as many as six thousand computations per second!

"This little comp board in the briefcase is experimental. It's about nine inches by fourteen inches and isn't more than three inches thick.

"We had to build a special generation plant in fifty. We had to control temperature and humidity exactly. Even a tiny change in atmospheric pressure could affect the thing.

"This one uses four common flashlight "C" batteries and works well at minus one hundred or plus two hundred, under water or with zero humidity and at pressures from a vacuum to a few thousand pounds per square inch! It also handles eighty four million plus computations per second as well as keeping the time, date and a storage of good music I can listen to through earphones. It picks up any radio or television station in the area and has a built-in modular phone. It keeps my appointments for months ahead and can automatically get me airline tickets and book me into hotels. It records anything I wish it to record.

"If you asked that fifties computer a stupid question like `How high is up?' it would blow a dozen fuses and need complete reprogramming. It would be out of service for a month.

"If you ask that question of this thing a voice will politely tell you to stop wasting time and effort on such stupid semantic questions, then it tells you high is relative to gravitic effects, except with drugs,, so once one has reached a point where such impulses become too weak to note you are beyond the concepts of up or down.

"I know. I asked it, just to see what would happen. That drug high reference was a shocker!

"Where does fire go when it goes out?

"It merely dissipates on a standard square-of-the-distance ratio unless absorbed by an energy or mass field.

"I know. I asked.

"How can you make a horse turn into a barn?

"Pull the reins on the side the barn lays and the horse will turn in that direction, with supposition the animal is properly trained. Stop playing semantic games.

"What is the capacity of the hotel's hot water heater?

"Why would anyone want to heat hot water?

"The damned thing has a sense of humor!

"It really seems that way, you know. It was a programmed response put in by the kid who makes the programs up for us.

"I asked it a question about the expected possible security problems concerning this new plant and its location last evening, using the standard term `Military intelligence' – and the damned thing said I'd used an oxymoron. There was no evidence in all of recorded history to indicate anything military *could* possess intelligence! It said to rephrase the question!

"What I'm trying to say is we can't know what new thing we'll come up with tomorrow, or even this afternoon. We have to be able to foresee the likelihood of all new innovations and new technologies and design our facilities around abstracts – *before* we invest the millions in construction or even in the land to build the place on. If I can discuss this directly with the directors of the departments concerned it would save us valuable time, which is saying, money. The department heads have experience in more things than their underlings. That's why they're department heads – at Crane.

"I also will want to talk with the chief planner on the construction and inspection board and with the head of the zoning department. We must resolve any problems before they arise or put in a mechanism that won't lose us a lot of valuable time while petty people make petty objections.

"We may decide the wall is unscalable and that Crane should look elsewhere to build this new facility.

"Putting it quite bluntly, Crane is *not* known as the kind

of company willing to put up with silly bureaucratic obstructionism from petty underlings."

That ruffled her feathers a bit, as it was designed to do. She was a typical bureaucrat sent to test me and to delay things. She was filled with a sense of her own vast importance and would respond in a more fixed manner than the little comp I was showing her.

"I imagine you've already found locations you've walked away from?" she asked, sweetly, a definite threat in her tone.

"No. This is my first choice. I do think you can understand how long the most senior bureaucrat would stay at her job if a memo letter from Crane were to inform the commission that this multimillion dollar facility – that would have paid enormous taxes and employed large numbers of highly paid specially educated professional personnel – would not be coming to that particular county because of that particular bureaucrat's obstructionism, can't you?

"I'm not going to spend a lot of time talking to someone who's *not* qualified to give me answers!"

I decided to make her hate me, because the commission had sent her to feel me out, and for no other reason. If she hated me, she would fear me. It was a strong part of the psychological type. I'd get fast results if I let her know in no uncertain terms I wouldn't hesitate to destroy her chances for any future advancement in her bureaucracy. It would also make her tell Pratz and DuMont that I was the type who thought a corporation like Crane could get anything it wanted with a few threats. That kind of business gives out bribes and threats in equal doses. My pigeons would certainly know that!

Miss Relski said she'd have the commission send people over who had the qualifications I demanded. She was a little snide, but I let it pass. She would have to consider what I actually might do to get her fired. She wouldn't waste too much time. Big business runs roughshod over the Miss Relskis of the world, but that was why she was where she was. The commission used her to learn about me and I used her to deliver a strong message she didn't have any idea she was carrying. She'd be miffed for a couple of days. In a week, I'd just be that unpleasant ass Crane sent. In a month, she'd forget I ever existed.

Well, under normal circumstances she would.

"Hello. I'm Kenneth Pratz and this is Tate DuMont," Pratz introduced. "We're here to discuss a plant Crane wants to build on the tract by the interstate? The Overton Tract?"

"Stan Carr," I said, offering my hand like a wet dead fish. "I need some more information on the place. I have to decide if it would be financially in our interests to locate here. Once we start, we tend to get larger and larger very quickly. I'll need solid assurances about what we can expect in several areas. I'll need to speak with someone from zoning, of course.

"I assume one of you is from the zoning board?"

"I'm head of the planning and suitability end," Pratz said. "I have to see that the comprehensive statewide plan isn't left out of these things too far. Tate's our building inspection and code enforcement chief. We work together on a lot of large projects to see that things proceed smoothly ... for everyone."

"I see. Maybe I should describe more or less what Crane

has in mind for this project. You can let me know if it's even feasible in this area.

"First, we want to build a facility that will cover more than thirty thousand square feet, in which we plan to produce a device for the pentagon. It's classified, so we'll have to screen anyone who works there or even walks inside the gates, once we get into production.

"There's a *very* small amount of waste byproduct that's been labeled as toxic, so we'll have to build some very expensive retaining and storage tanks and will have to arrange removal of those containers at some future date – if they ever get filled.

"I mention that because the construction of the storage vats is *very* expensive, so we'll have to know exactly what we face as to the specific construction codes we'll have to meet. The wastes will be produced for a very few years and only in extremely small quantities, then we'll modify the line to produce something else. It's on a very limited production basis, due to its nature – which I can't further discuss.

"We'll expand the space all the time. We always seem to be short of space for these top secret things. That's why I'm interested in this tract. It leaves us three times the projected space demands.

"I notice your Miss Plotnik or whatever told you which tract I have in mind."

"It seems you managed to turn her thoroughly against you," Pratz said. "She's a little scared of Crane or she'd tie things up for months."

"I fully intended to alienate her. It must be shown from the first step that Crane doesn't put up with a lot of stupid bureaucratic crap. I can see that anyone who tries to play those games with us will find it hard to ever find a job in any public contact area again. I want it established from the first that I resent the commission sending someone to discuss such matters who has none of the qualifications needed to deal with this project. Crane deals only with the top and buys only the best. We don't tolerate obstructionism. We decide what we require in a given situation, then we go straight to the heart of the matter. Delays and obstructions cost money, and that's what being in business is all about, isn't it?"

"Yeah. Making a living is why any of us work," DuMont agreed. "What is this about toxic waste? We can't let something be stored in the area that's going to start killing people a few years down the road!"

"It's mostly the cleaner compounds used in finishing certain micro- components. They *may* cause lung cancer in chronic smokers – who Crane does *not* employ as electronic component workers for the obvious reasons – if they eat six pounds of the crap a day for forty years or something as totally damned ludicrous. You know how extreme that sort of thing gets."

"Obvious reasons? Six pounds a day for forty years?" DuMont asked. "Are you serious?"

"The obvious reason is that tars that collect on the skin, in the hair, on the clothes and so forth of chronic smokers will contaminate delicate microcircuitry. Six pounds a day for forty years is approximately the dosage they gave the rats to see if they'd develop anything. The increase in cancer was one in seven thousand in even those doses – which is about triple the normal incidence.

"If we employ the three hundred people projected and they each eat six pounds of the stuff a day – incidentally, we'll produce about six pounds of it every three months! – one of them will develop cancer every forty years – if any of them were smokers. *Chain* smokers, yet!

"Now! You tell *me*! If you employ three hundred people, wouldn't you expect more than one case of cancer in forty years without *any* toxic waste being produced? (I started getting excited to the point of raving.) I'm surprised they don't declare oxygen a hazardous product! After all, it causes almost *all* the fires in the entire damned *world*! It's so damned *stupid*!

"Sorry. All that stuff costs a lot of money and doesn't really mean anything real! Some asshole of a so-called scientist wants his picture in the paper. `Publish or perish,' I think they call it."

"Ain't that the truth?" Pratz threw in. "They're wrong about half of it, anyhow. Twenty years after they outlaw something they find it was something like asbestos in the ceiling in the lab that caused the whole original mess, anyhow, not in the drinking water – that caused one case of cancer more than projected in fifty million people!

"The area out there, including the Ledderman and Milton tracts as well as the Overton site, are already zoned for light industry and agriculture. I can possibly pull a few strings to get the zoning variance you need. After all, it's government top secret work and you surely can't put it in a regular industrial park.

"Relski said the Overton Tract, so that's easy. You could even buy the other two parcels and would be in the middle of a very large area where security could be cheap. There are a few swamps that you can probably get exemption permits to fill if you're doing government contract work. Cypress swamps aren't exactly rare around here.

"I'll have to see if the county will allow the added expense to my budget for it. They should be happy to spend the money if it'll bring in more jobs and taxes. (Raise the inflection of the voice and an eyebrow. Gee! I wonder what he means?!) I can bet the salaries for most of those people won't be minimum wage. It's not like it's so much when you consider the scope of the project. A few lousy thousand bucks shouldn't stop them. It will take only until they approve the funds and read it into the record. Two to three months."

This was it! That was as much as a request for a bribe in the way it was worded and the little expressions.

"Three months? No. That's not acceptable. Crane doesn't wait any three months. I doubt they'll wait three weeks. Time is money. When we decide to do a thing, we do it *now*, not at some vague date in the future.

"Mr. Grimes, the major owner of Crane, lives in Sarasota or somewhere close like that. I think I even saw where he owns some land close to Naples, so maybe he can get involved and expedite matters, though we'd prefer he doesn't. He tends to overly take charge of a project, if he gets involved. He won't usually have anything to do with the running of the businesses, but I may be able to talk him into something."

"He's the *detective* who solved that art thing a few weeks ago, isn't he?" Pratz said, staring hard at DuMont.

"Yeah. It drives the board crazy for him to spend so much of his time on that silliness. He should be running the company! Time is money! Who the hell cares who knocks off some local cheap whore?

"I guess when you're worth eight billion dollars you can do pretty much what you want, but a few lousy dollars spread around in the right places can save a hell of a lot of money, in the long run. Grimes has so damned much money he doesn't have the least conception of how important it is in the way the world runs.

"Well, we peasants have to get along as best we can.

"We have to get this show on the road. We have to find a way to expedite this local-yokel political bumbling about funds that are no more than the taxes they'll collect in no more than a few days, once this operation gets moving!"

"Perhaps Crane will produce those few funds?" Pratz asked with a very studied look on his face.

"I don't see why not – if they're within reason. We have some funds to, er, to use to, uh, research the various phases of these kinds of rapid growth operations. Expediting funds.

"What amount do you think will be needed to, as the funds are for, further expedite this project? What kind of guarantees will I have?"

"I'll have to figure exactly what it'll cost to convince the county board to get this handled in a day or two, if you get the drift. Usually a couple of thousand will more than convince them there's a need to hurry a specific thing. I'll have to pay a certain secretary to go through her files and happen to place the item on that day's agenda with a certified study for recommendation to pass it without further discussion from my department.

"I'll put in a long list of supposed tests and studies and legal opinions. I keep a bunch of them around that only need the name and legal description of the tract filled in. Nobody ever reads any of it. It's a bunch of words that don't mean anything to anyone without an advanced degree – and none of that bunch even finished high school, judging by the way they do things.

"I won't mince words with you. I'll expect to be rewarded very handsomely for my personal help in expediting this matter."

"I know a bribe proposal when I hear it!" I snapped, shortly. "How much? Total? What the hell do you think an expediting fund *is*!?"

He grinned at me, and said, "It's refreshing to know we won't we won't have to sit around playing children's games about this. How much will your fund spring for?"

"That depends on how many times I'll have to dip into it. I'll be as frank with both of you as you are with me. We don't want to have to spend all that money on those stupid containment vats like they were supposed to hold plutonium or some kind of nuclear crap! The vats are to hold stuff that's not known to be dangerous in any way, it just *might* be very minimally dangerous if you eat six pounds of it a day for forty years. It's not nerve gas, for god's sake!

"That's your department, Mr. DuMont. The ball's in your court. Give me a figure."

"Uh, how big a part is it?" DuMont asked.

"We have to build a couple of vats. Maybe two thousand gallons or a little more, apiece. If we could put in some large septic tanks and seal off the outflow pipes, it would do the trick. Crane will be there for decades. There won't be any danger to anyone else. I say there isn't any danger to anyone, anywhere! *I'll* be at that plant, myself, a lot of the time!"

"Well, I could show you a way to put the containment vats on the plans that would allow me to inspect them as septic tanks and you could say that was a code because of the secret nature of the business," DuMont suggested. "I could then inspect them as septic tanks and pass them as septic tanks, then you could seal off the drain lines or you could actually seal off the outflow pipes from the inside and lay a standard drain line for me to inspect. I don't check *inside* the tanks! I'll handle all the inspections there, personally, and there won't be any trouble, at all. That's my guarantee."

"There may be other phases where inspections could be less than, er, *extreme,* that will possiblyarise. I see I can work with you. I need definite figures to be able to tap the fund."

"A flat ten thousand will do for me," DuMont replied. "I'm not a major expense, you see. You'll save a hundred times that, just in the containment vats. Any future deals will be made then and aren't included."

"I have to pay off others," Pratz said. "I'd say seventy five grand, cash, old unseriesed bills."

"I can't go that high. That much would lose me the advantages of the area. It would also cut into my own, er, commissions."

"I see. You can't get Grimes to pay enough for you to get your little cut for yourself," Pratz said with a sneer.

"Oh, good lord! If Mr. Grimes ever had any hint we do business this way he'd have the whole lot of us in the pen! *He* doesn't know anything at all, except that Crane wants to build a plant!"

"Sixty grand. Not a penny less," Pratz said. "Half down and half when the OK comes through. Same deal with Tate."

"How soon can this be done?"

"As soon as I have the money, it'll start, and will be done

in three days. Guaranteed!"

"I'll buy the land this afternoon and will meet you two here at nine in the morning," I said, closing the briefcase. "Good day – and don't let me down. It wouldn't be smart."

I walked out as soon as they drove off, got into my rented car and headed for the Sarasota plant. The little recorder in the case was of voicecoder quality. The little wide-angle video camera, I hoped, had been focused to get it all at the same time. Crane makes those things for the FBI and CIA, so they weren't hard for me to get. I didn't have any warrants, but I didn't plan to use the material in court, so that didn't matter. I'd have a warrant and surveillance by Sam and Dan when I handed Pratz and DuMont bribes, in the morning. Then I'd have the handle I'd need to solve the murder. Pratz and DuMont weren't the type to take that fall!

"As soon as you hand them the money we'll step in and tag the slimy bastards," Sam said. "We have the warrants and a certain friend of yours, a *very* prominent judge, got a `for cause' warrant so we can use the tapes you already made. You were acting in your official capacity as a marshal for the grand jury – if you're ever asked. There's no reason to believe that stuff will ever come up, but we like to be protected just as much as those crooks do!

"The room's set up beautifully. The hotel's a good one and this suite's a good place for this to be going down. I can be in the bedroom and Dan can be in that big closet. They'll be here in about an hour, so we have time."

"They'll be here in half an hour or maybe a little less. That's why I had you two get here so early. They'll want to come early so we won't have time to prepare – in case this is exactly what it is. They're used to taking bribes and they know how to cover themselves – in most situations. Think like a crook to catch a crook!"

We finished our breakfast and took away the extra dishes. I didn't doubt my two pigeons would check to be sure there were no extras sent to the rooms and that the rooms to either side had unsuspicious people in them.

They showed up forty minutes early. I was in pajamas, cup of coffee and Danish on the coffee table and papers spread around the room in neat little stacks, according to content. I grunted when they came in and let them sit while I called Tony Jacobi at the Sarasota plant. If they'd checked the number (They had. DuMont watched me punch the number and nodded at Pratz) they'd know the call *was* to Crane. I got the switchboard and asked to speak with Mr. Jacobi, told the operator my phony name, waited a minute, then discussed the so-called project with him for a few minutes. I handed the phone to Pratz for him to listen to Tony tell him he'd better consider very carefully before trying to pull any fast deals with Crane, which had several billions of dollars at its disposal to straighten out rough spots or to eliminate any problems that might arise on any such projects. Tony can sound like a very hardened hood, when he wants to. I could see he scared hell out of Pratz.

Pratz gave me back the phone and I asked if it was approved that I go ahead and disburse the funds, then hung up.

"Let's get this all perfectly understood before we go any further. I want you to spell out exactly what each of us will deliver in return for the money or services of the other. I don't want anyone to come back later and try to claim something was or was not included. Not you and not me.

I'm sure Mr. Jacobi made Crane's position in the matter very clear."

"He said, we cross Crane, we feed the fish in the bay or maybe the Caloosahatchee River, and Crane's got a few billion laying around to make damned sure we do," Pratz said.

"Mr. Jacobi did *not* say anything like that!"

"He said some things about business relations and how unwise it would be for any person to fail to honor a contract with Crane, verbal or written. I got the message, loud and clear. That's no problem.

"For the sum of sixty thousand dollars, half of which I am to receive now and half on delivery of what I agree on, I will see that you get the permits, studies, releases and acceptances of the commission within five days of this date. Fair enough?"

"And your bribe, as earlier agreed, includes all funds that will be needed or asked? You guarantee there will be no future need of funds to ensure our immediate use of the parcels under discussion?"

"I guarantee it!"

"And you, Mr. DuMont? For your own payment of ten thousand dollars on the same schedule as that of Mr. Pratz, what guarantees do I have?"

"All we talked about was containment vats!" DuMont answered, quickly. "I didn't say anything about any other problems! You have to guarantee you won't dump a bunch more stuff on me! For the ten grand you get to put in the septic tanks and call them vats and I'll guarantee their inspection and passage. Period! That's all we talked about!"

"That's true. If we need any other codes not to be

enforced we'll make a separate deal at that time. Your bribe is solely concerned with no more than three containment vats. That should cover it, I think. I'll expect those permits and papers in no more than five days. Here's your money. Thirty grand for Pratz and five for DuMont. Count it. The rest will come on the completion of contracts, as agreed."

Dumont stuck his envelope in an inner pocket, but Pratz almost drooled as he opened the briefcase to look at the stacks of old twenties and fifties. He took a few packets out and put them back in, then closed the case and said I'd hear from him a bit later in the day to get the full reading of my documentary stamps and so forth from the titles to the property for use in the legal descriptions on the permits.

"Come in, Mr. Pratz, Dumont," I greeted. "I may assume you have completed our contract, as promised?"

"Here're the plans and approval certificates," Pratz answered, and handed me the folder of papers.

"And here's your second half of the bribe," I replied, handing him the case of money and DuMont an envelope.

"It's been a pleasure doing busi ... what in hell?!?" Pratz cried, as Sam and Dan stepped into the room with their service revolvers aimed right between the eyes of the two.

"Good work, CD!" Sam said, then read them their rights, served the warrants, and explained that I was CD Grimes, state grand jury field operative, and was helping them in their investigation of corruption, bribery and other crimes.

"There's one further little charge for me to add to the bribery and conspiracy charges," Sam finished. "Murder one!"

"Murder?!" DuMont cried. "What are you talking about? Murder?!"

"The murder of one Edward Zimmer. We found the video of you two, Reynolds, and a hood named Moreni passing a bribe at the construction site. This scam was to be able to prove it *was* bribery. We've proved beyond the possibility of any doubt that you two *do* take bribes. You have no defense, whatever. It'll be damned easy to show you killed Zimmer to get that video tape."

"But I didn't have anything to do with killing anyone!" DuMont wailed. "I didn't know anything about it until I heard he was found in the bay!"

"Moreni's from Detroit and wouldn't know how to find some local yokel hick who took a video at a construction site," Dan said. "P. P. Reynolds is probably in the same situation, so far as that goes. You can bet he'll have an alibi we can't hope to break, so you two'll goat for him.

"Zimmer couldn't reach Reynolds to try a little blackmail, but he'd damned well know all about you. He *was* a construction worker who probably saw you a hundred times around jobs. You have nothing!"

"But we *all* saw him taking those pictures! All of us!" Pratz cried. "Reynolds or Moreni could either one have done it. I was sure as hell a long way from this area when he was killed. I can prove it. You can't prove a thing against me!"

"We can damned well prove you take bribes and that you knew he had the pictures and that you're in a position to have located him and a hundred other things," Sam pointed out, dryly. "You're what we have and what we can present to a jury. I think the two of you will get the chair for this, because people are going to be sore as all hell about the bribes, and people are what make up a jury. Those same people are paying your salaries, as will be pointed out to them a number of times while you're on trial. You'd be wise to not say anything else until you have legal advice."

"I'm not going to take any murder charge for anyone!" DuMont snarled. "I didn't have anything to do with any killing! Ken *was* here at the time of the murder! He set up his alibi in Punta Gorda, but he *wasn't* there playing poker with that bunch, at all! I heard him on the phone telling them to claim he was there! He was right here the whole time!"

That was a bit more than we'd hoped for! DuMont was already in a panic. We wouldn't have to put a lot of extra pressure on him to break him.

Chapter three

"It sort of surprised me when DuMont shot down the alibi our Mr. Pratz had all set up," Sam said. "I guess the first thing those kind of crooks always do is try to cover their own tails. I think we can count on DuMont making a deal, if he can, but it's not enough to make Pratz the actual killer. Not to where we can prove it."

"It was most probably a hired job," Dan agreed. "My money's on Moreni. He'd be the first person to call in muscle, he'd know who to call, and that's just business as usual to his type.

"We do have one very big problem though. It has to do with that three fifty seven magnum. There's no way the ones who heard firecrackers being fired off that close wouldn't have heard that cannon a lot louder!"

"There weren't any firecrackers. If you check, you'll find there were less than half a dozen of those so-called firecracker noises. The powder burns will show how it was done. What we're going to have trouble with is finding which one of our suspects hired him killed – or did the job himself."

"You don't agree it was Moreni?" Dan asked.

"It might have been. Our big snag is proving it. The murder was awfully soon after he was seen taking the pictures, and Moreni wouldn't know any local talent. There wasn't time to get anyone down here from New York. He could have gotten someone from Miami or Tampa, but that's still pushing it. The timing's against us, on that."

"I think we can eliminate DuMont," Sam put in. "He very simply doesn't have the guts. I'll let you read the statement he made as soon as it's typed up and signed and I can make copies.

"You weren't here for that one!"

"He really spilled his guts about the bribes," Dan agreed. "Pratz isn't saying a word about anything and refuses to make any statement, whatever."

"Which could very well be a clever act to make us think DuMont doesn't have the guts to be involved in murder."

"I sort of thought about that point," Sam said. "I've seen enough of his type to know he really *doesn't* have the guts for it."

"I'll read what he said later. I'm going to Sarasota to give Tony the spy equipment back and to have a bunch of legal transcriptions made for court. I'll be back late this afternoon, late. You can give me the transcript of DuMont's testimony and we can see what we can use.

"I'm going to tell Lydia and Lou to go ahead with the story about the bribes. They can use Reynolds and Moreni can't they? Did DuMont tag them?"

"And *how*!" Dan exclaimed.

"I'll get Lydia. She's out front, as usual," Sam said, and went out of the office to return with Lydia. After a few minutes we agreed on what could be printed. Sam hadn't told anyone else about any of it because of our agreement with her.

She went out to phone in her scoop and I took my Jeep to head for Sarasota. Crane was going to give the courts some evidence so damning even some of the idiotic judges we have in the system weren't going to be able to find any way to let the politicians out of this one!

"This is what he said for the record," Sam said, handing

me a legal copy of DuMont's statement. "See if you can find anything we can use to put pressure on anyone for anything other than the bribery part.

"We caught friend Moreni trying to board a plane for New York and informed him it would be most unwise for him to try to leave the area again – unless he wanted to spend the time we were finishing our investigation in jail because we feel he's a strong risk to skip bond. I have a man watching him every minute."

The statement was purely disgusting to me in the way DuMont was trying to make himself appear a victim of circumstances, but it was really going to land Pratz in for the long haul:

Dumont: It started about four years ago. I was recently promoted to my present position. There was that mall over on Shady Pine Boulevard that T. T. Middling was building. I saw right away that everything was decidedly under code. I hung red tags on all of it – plumbing, electrical, drywall, roof joists, doors – you name it. Nothing was up to code. Mr. Pratz and Mr. DeJulius came to my office and argued that there was already an agreement about the construction made by my predecessor. I argued the code wasn't something my predecessor or anyone else could waive.

Q: There's no record that you ever reported those breaches of regulations. Why did you not report the fact your predecessor was not properly enforcing the Southern Building Code?

DuMont: Because Kenneth Pratz explained that Mr. Wallings, my former boss, was dying of prostate cancer and that he had made the agreements in this one case in return for which Mr. DeJulius would guarantee to take care of Mr. Wallings' family, his wife and daughter and his invalid mother for the rest of their lives or until the wife or daughters married. If I didn't honor that agreement Mr. Wallings' crime would be known and his family would have nothing, as even his pension would be declared null and void. I said I'd have to go along with it, but it was not to happen again or I'd be forced to expose the whole sordid thing.

Q: You are saying the mall is not now and was never up to code?

DuMont: No it isn't. There are already great problems with leaks in the roof and window and door frames that are not properly centered or of sufficient strength to withstand normal stresses. The older paving is breaking up and will all have to be redone. Also, the plumbing has never worked properly. There have been three or four electrical fires and the lights often go off for no apparent reason. There are other complaints.

Q: You continued to allow code violations on other sites?

DuMont: I had no choice. Once I did it that first time they had me. If I refused anything else they demanded I would end up in jail.

Q: Did you receive payment for overlooking violations?

DuMont: If I was going to do it anyhow I might as well be paid for it. It was the same thing if I was paid or not. Mr. Pratz said they would trust me if I took their money and wouldn't turn me in because they were scared of what I might do.

"Sounds like Reagan and Bush still blaming all the world's problems on Carter, doesn't it?" I said.

"That now seems to be the American Way," Dan agreed, with a grin and a wink.

Q: You told Det. Lukens that Mr. Pratz was not up in Punta Gorda, that you overheard him speaking on the telephone with someone in an attempt to establish an alibi for the time when Mr. Edward Murray Zimmer was killed, did you not?

DuMont: That is correct, though I can't swear certainly it was to establish an alibi for the time Zimmer was killed. There is some possibility he wanted an alibi for some other reason. It merely occurred to me that it was for the murder later. I had no hint about that at that time.

Q: Do you know with whom Mr. Pratz was speaking on the office phone when he was trying to establish a false alibi?

DuMont: No. He talked with Mr. Reynolds and Mr. Moreni in the hall for a few minutes, they left and he came inside and called someone. He only said he wanted to talk with Harry when he made the call. I didn't hear him say any other name.

"I see Reynolds and Moreni are still neck deep in it. One or both of them suggested he establish an alibi – or was the conversation about something else? Maybe a report to Reynolds and Moreni that he'd killed Zimmer?"

"It gets even better," Sam smirked. "Read on."

Q: This was when? The morning after the body was found in the bay?

DuMont: It was that morning, but it was before we had opened the offices.

Q: Do you open those offices at 9:30 AM like most such public offices?

DuMont: No. We deal with construction. We open to the public at 8:30, but we're required to be there at 8:00. This was, oh, about a quarter to eight.

Q: But the body wasn't even reported until a few minutes after nine when it was brought in. My records say the first information was made public at 9:21 AM. How did you know about it?

DuMont: It was the first I knew (pause) about 10:30. My secretary called me on the radio in my car and said a construction worker on the Reynolds job had been found dead, or they thought it was a worker there or something, because there wasn't any confirmed identification yet. All I know is that Mr. Pratz called someone in Punta Gorda named Harry and said that Harry was to identify him as being there playing poker from 10:00 in the evening until 4 AM. Harry was to get three others to swear to it. I didn't have any idea what the alibi was for at the time and assumed Mr. Pratz might have been in some place where he was not supposed to be so needed an alibi to avoid trouble with his wife. He messes around sometimes. You can guess how shocked I was to later discover it was the same person who took our pictures who was dead and that Mr. Pratz was going to such extremes to establish an alibi for just that time. When I heard about the worker's deat, it didn't connect. Not even when I had both things (pause) you know. It didn't connect at the time. When they said he was killed and that the time of death was (pause) when it was, I became very frightened.

Q: Why didn't you immediately report your suspicions to the police.

DuMont: Yeah. Right. (Sarcastically and with facial expression denoting sarcasm) My picture was there, too. I would end up in jail if I wasn't also killed to shut me up.

Q: You are saying you didn't report the false alibi because you feared for your own life?

DuMont: That is correct.

Q: You had some reason to believe Mr. Pratz was a killer?

DuMont: (Excitedly) No. I have every reason to believe Mr. Moreni is a killer and he's right in the middle of all this. He's a member of a gang of (pause) I guess you'd call them organized criminals. From New York or Detroit ... maybe Cleveland. The papers call them the Farris Franchise. Mr. Moreni was here in their behalf to meet with Mr. Reynolds. They never made a secret of it and Mr. Moreni actually bragged about knowing the whole Farris family and claimed to have worked for them, mainly Frank and Tom, since he was 17 years old. Mr. Reynolds fronts for them here. They build all these expensive subdivisions and malls and business office buildings to launder money.

Q: You know that for a certainty?

DuMont: I sure do. They talked about it all the time and about what happened to people who 'got in their way,' as they put it.

"He goes on telling about the Farris Franchise and how they work here," Sam said, over my shoulder. "If he has all the records he says he has, he'll get a deal and relocation from the US witness protection program. The important thing to us is how he tied Moreni into it so tight. He certainly established ample solid motive and opportunity for Pratz, directly, and for Moreni and Reynolds, indirectly. He also gave evidence they all had intimate knowledge about such interesting little details as time of death long before they reasonably could have had that knowledge.

"I know they'll set something up that'll establish an alibi for that time, but we can bring this in, no matter what, since it's been volunteered. No jury will swallow too long a series of coincidences – scratch that! You never know what a jury will do!"

"Ain't that the truth?" Dan said, coming in from the hall. "I could tell you some stories!

"CD, you promised you'd explain about the firecracker noise coming from a three fifty seven by the powder burn pattern. It's time to do that or half our case for the murder being committed at Coconut Road is down the drain. If the people at the fish camp heard the firecrackers, they'd sure as hell hear that cannon. If there'd been a silencer used, they wouldn't have heard anything at that distance."

"Were the powder burns in a perfectly circular pattern on a small area around the hole?"

"Yeah," Dan replied. "The coroner mentioned that."

"Let's go into the test room and I'll show you how it was done, then why they fired several times will become evident. They wanted it to sound like firecrackers."

Sam grinned and raised an eyebrow at me, then led us to the ballistics room. Dan carried in a .357 and filled out a form to explain the circumstances under which the gun was to be fired. He has to account for every bullet used.

"I'm putting it down as scientific noise suppression tests of high caliber pistol fire for court use. I assume it *will* be used for that?"

"Uh-huh. I need a piece of pipe."

"All I got is two inch PVC," the technician offered.

"Fine. About two feet of it. It's generally what's used for this trick, anyhow.

The technician looked through a scrap bin while I set up a tape recorder next to the ballistics box and another across the room. I handed a third to Dan and said to take it out into the hall and to turn it on when I called out, saying it was a noise suppression test and giving his location where he was standing and noting there was a closed door between to simulate distance.

Sam handed me a piece of PVC pipe about twenty inches long.

I called out for Dan to start his recorder, then turned on my own two recorders, made a speech about the location and purpose of the test, put the end of the pistol in the pipe, aimed into the ballistics box, pulled the trigger four times, paused, and fired again. I then called out for Dan to come back inside the room with his recorder. We rewound the tapes back to the start and turned on the one nearest the box. My words came on to explain the test, then there was a loud retort that almost blew the speaker out in the little recorder.

I let it run past the sounds, punched the record button and said, "The sound of the pistol was directed through the pipe close to this recorder. Distance – approximately forty inches away, thus we hear the full retort of a three fifty seven magnum shot."

I then turned on the recorder from across the room and said to note the degree the noise was suppressed to the side, even in the same room. I estimated the distance was about fifteen feet. It sounded like a large firecracker. Close.

Dan turned on his own recorder and ran it to the shots. They sounded exactly like cherry bomb firecrackers being set off at a distance. Dan made the explanations into that machine, then we turned the tapes and machines over to the technician for sealing and authentication while we went back to Sam's office.

"You can see how it was done and why the burn pattern was so important. That shows the killer was experienced in this kind of killing. It's a trick I learned from an Interpol officer a long time ago. If you don't have a silencer, this is next best."

"I think this will tie Moreni into it," Sam said. "That's only to us. It's not something you could give a jury. We'd first have to prove Moreni's ties to the Farris Franchise and organized crime. If we had that solidly done he'd already be in the pen. We can't actually prove anything against the gang – yet.

"We have a method that stinks of Moreni and we have the sudden need for Pratz to have an alibi before the body was even reported publicly."

"So either Moreni did the actual killing or he coached our own Mr. Pratz," Dan said. "Maybe Moreni killed him and Pratz drove the getaway car."

"I think probably Moreni and Pratz pulled him over onto that median and forced him into their own car," Sam agreed. "Pratz was driving. They took Zimmer out Coconut Road, simply because it was close, he wouldn't listen to what passes for reason among those types, so Moreni shot him, then the two of them dumped the body into the canal, Moreni fired a few more shots through the pipe so no one would investigate the single shot too soon, they drove off and Zimmer floated out with the tide. The only thing we can't do is prove one word of it, but it had to be that way! It *had* to!"

"I agree. I think I can get proof enough to be able to convince a jury. I just have to figure some kind of scam to work it. I have an idea. It'll work if the trash hasn't been picked up, yet."

"The trash?" Dan asked.

I grinned and headed out the door. I had to check out a couple of things and I had to hope. Something as simple as a trash collection could screw things up pretty badly.

The Jeep's good for shortcuts. I was able to cut through a dirt path through a patch where punk trees had been removed to get on Metro, where I made good time getting to the county branch offices. I first went through the Dumpster outside. It hadn't been emptied in a couple of days, but there wasn't anything in it I was looking for. I went through the storage areas around the complex, but found only a couple of pieces of pipe that would fit what I was looking for. I carefully put a tag on each one, stating it was for court evidence and was not to be touched, but I knew none of those were what I was looking for, then went into the offices and checked around for a bit, after the secretary spoke with Sam on the phone. Sam had her tell me he was having the entire route along Coconut Road and back to the hotel where Moreni was staying checked. The hotel's Dumpsters were being searched. He gave me Pratz's address so I could check there.

Nothing.

I didn't think anyone would be stupid enough to keep the pipe, but I didn't know where else to look, so I had the foreman open the trunk of the car Pratz had been driving the past few days. There was a piece of one and three quarters PVC pipe a little more than two feet long over the jack stand. I called Sam and told him to send the print and lab crew over.

Now to get the evidence sewed so tight they couldn't hope to get around it. They screwed up good here, but not the way one might think!

Chapter four

"Breaker one nine for that Truth Sleuth. You got your ears on?"

I picked up the microphone and replied, "Ten four, Tar Burner. What it is?"

"Twenty at stopover. Pronto," Dan ordered.

He wanted me to come to the office, fast? What had happened?

I turned back across the cleared field to Metro and was at the station in a few minutes. Dan was standing by the crime lab van, helping them load some equipment. He nodded at the officers and came to the Jeep.

"Sam's already there. I'll ride out with you and come back with him. It seems poor Mr. Pratz has met with a most unfortunate kind of freak accident. He seems to have fallen off a scaffolding on one of the highrises friend Reynolds is building over by the interstate."

"Where's Moreni?"

"He's locked in his room at the motel. He hasn't left his room since Sam explained the facts of life to him. We can't tie this one to him."

"I think maybe we're looking in the wrong place on this thing all along. There's a crew going over the car Pratz used."

"And?"

"The pipe's right there in the trunk. It's a bit too pat."

"Uh-huh. I felt we were getting a bit too much from Mr. DuMont, all along, but he can't be involved in a frame or in the accident that won't be. He's sitting in a cell," Dan pointed out.

"His frame was only that story about Pratz and his dud alibi. There's something else missing in all this – like what was Pratz doing out?"

"His bond was posted. P. P. Reynolds is the only something else we have."

"Surely someone's watching *him*!"

"Yeah. That means he's out for this one – except he could have hired some hand to handle it for him."

"I feel more and more that we're missing something obvious. I've wondered all along why Zimmer had that video camera out there. Construction workers don't go around making videos of their everyday work. It isn't making much sense that he would have the thing there to make that tape."

"I agree. There's something we don't know, yet. There's Sam."

We pulled up to a barricade and went to find Pratz laying in a wad under a broken scaffolding stand. He had apparently fallen three stories. I looked over the scene.

"When did it happen? Any witnesses?"

"About half an hour ago. The crew around on the other side heard him yell and came around to find him."

I looked upward to study the hanging planks. The scaffolding was suspended on four cables, one of which had snapped (Or been taken loose, as was actually the case), suddenly dropping one end of the platform.

"Funny how that thing flipped over to the side, yet he fell straight down under it."

"There's a rope rail around it," a worker said. "He'd have grabbed it and tried to hang on. He'd drop straight down if he couldn't hold it."

"And hit head first?"

The body was against the base of the wall in a tangle. One side of his head was caved in.

The worker shrugged.

"It's also a bit strange he hit on the side of his head like that without even getting his nice new shirt dirty on the shoulder that would have had to hit at the same time. It's funny the only damage seems to be to the side of his head. Wanna bet there aren't any of Pratz's fingerprints anywhere on that scaffolding?"

"What? You sayin' somebody croaked him right there, then fixed the riser to look like he was dumped?" the worker said. "Some union feud or somethin'?"

"You got it! Somethin'!"

We waited until the coroner came to look things over. Sam and Dan spent the time asking questions of the workers, but it was as obvious as it could be there was no accident. Pratz was killed to shut him up.

DuMont had worked his own frame of Pratz in his own way, but I thought that was nothing more than saving his own tail feathers.

After a single glance, the coroner declared he damned well didn't fall off of that scaffolding lift, then he did a quick cursory. "I'd say his head was bashed in with something about two inches square, which makes one of the drywall hammers a good bet. I'll have a report this afternoon. Prelim, anyhow."

Sam and Dan headed for the office and I started home, then went to the office myself to study that tape again. We hadn't paid a lot of attention to the first part because we'd jumped on the Pratz/DuMont part and concentrated on the bribery exchange scenes.

Zimmer had spent a lot of time taking pictures of the

general area from various angles, showing the house with the 34 on the side several times as people went in and out. He managed to show several cars and trucks coming and going in the short time before the exchange with our prize-winning humanitarians. It seemed to me he was very interested in that place, and the bribery thing seemed to happen when he was following Moreni and Reynolds back out of the house. He would focus now and then on a car or truck, so we might have a clue in that.

"See anything" Dan asked, handing me a cup of coffee.

"Maybe,. It seems there was a lot of traffic into the house with the black thirty four on it. Moreni and Reynolds went in and were then being followed with the camera as they came back out. They met with Pratz and DuMont and he started panning around a bit, then suddenly heard or saw something and changed the focus back to them. He saw them move around and probably heard them arguing. He moved barely in time to get it on the tape. If he'd been there to get that meeting, he wouldn't have been anywhere they'd see him. He probably took that videotape because it suddenly started happening right there. He was there to take pictures of something about that house."

"Yeah. I was thinking something along those lines. See how this strikes you.

"Zimmer saw some drug deal going down at that job and made an anonymous tip to us. I went out there, but couldn't get anything. He decided to get his own proof. While he was getting that on tape, Reynolds and Moreni met Pratz and DuMont, so he went to that and ended up dead.

"That means he either didn't get the evidence he was after before the bribe or we don't know it when we're looking at it."

"That's about how I figure it. The killing still revolves around Reynolds and Moreni. Moreni isn't in any position to be able to do the job himself, but he damned well knows who to hire, how, and the rest of it.

"He has one big problem: Reynolds. There isn't time to get a hit man called in. Zimmer has that bribery tape and will turn it in before they can get muscle in from Detroit, New York, or Miami.

"Reynolds starts pushing hard, so Moreni gets together with Pratz and they knock Zimmer over. DuMont spills his damned guts and even throws his part of it back on Pratz. Moreni's being watched and can't get out of the area. Pratz is going to be put into a position where he'll have to talk or end up in the chair. Pratz will have to go – and Reynolds knows how to handle that! Moreni *told* him how to do it and who to get.

"Reynolds has ties with the Farris Franchise, gets a pro in to get rid of Pratz, and bails Pratz out. The hit's made and the hit man's already well on his way back to New York or wherever. DuMont is both out of reach and not very dangerous, because he's managed to blab so much he won't be believed.

"That means Moreni has to go, because we're going to be able to break him down. We have to watch that one very carefully."

"We can break Moreni down. We can't touch Reynolds, now. He's too powerful, and we don't have nearly enough evidence yet to more than tag him with the bribery bit. He'll get away with that by paying a fine and being oh so contrite for the judge and the nice people on the jury, then it's back to business as usual at seven sharp the next morning."

"Which puts us in a very strange position."

"What strange position?" Sam asked, coming from the back room.

"We have no usable motive for Reynolds. Reynolds is our only viable suspect, if we've figured this thing at all correctly – this time."

"We've got him for bribery. Cold!" Sam said.

"We showed bribery doesn't mean anything to his type when we set Pratz and DuMont up," Dan said, getting a surprised look from Sam, then a thoughtful one.

"Damn! Here's what Earl said on the coroner's report."

I looked it over and nodded. Pratz didn't fall, which we'd already shown.

"They didn't attempt to hide the fact this was a hit," Dan said. "That has to point right to Reynolds and Moreni. There isn't any other way. It doesn't make sense!"

"So. Somebody wants Reynolds and Moreni tagged," Sam decided.

"Which means Zimmer knew about something all along. I still think Moreni and Pratz killed Zimmer."

"So somebody else thinks Zimmer has something on the tape and wants this case closed before we find it," Sam agreed. "Pratz and Moreni were suckered into killing Ed Zimmer, solving everyones' problems."

"Now they have to get rid of the rest of the problem that we wouldn't know existed if it wasn't for the fact none of this crap makes much sense," I said. "What we have is the fact the whole bunch of them were either in on some other deal or they knew enough to hang somebody. Killing Pratz that way was designed to put Moreni right in the middle of it, so I can guess he's the only one who *doesn't* know what's going on."

"Him and maybe Reynolds," Sam added. "I hate to think that slimy scumball bastard may be innocent of most of this!"

"Let's go see Moreni. We can lay it all right on the line for him. He might know something they don't know he knows. We can make a deal. They *have* to kill him before we can show he doesn't know anything. If we ever discover that, we won't close this case. The idea is, with him dead, we'll forget the whole thing – if they do it right."

We got in Sam's car and went to the hotel. The deputy on guard said Moreni hadn't come out of his room. He'd had his breakfast sent in.

We knocked. No answer.

"If you've let him give you the slip I'll see you walking a beat in the worst damned part of this county!" Sam snarled at the deputy.

"I swear!" the deputy cried. "He never came out of that room since I came on at five this morning! The only one who went in or came out was room service! The same one came out who went in each time!"

"Each time?" I said, perking up.

"The boy brought the breakfast at seven forty and came back for the dishes at eight ten. The other one brought a pot of coffee and rolls at ten thirty."

"Oh, hell! He wouldn't get coffee and rolls that soon after breakfast!"

"Was the guy who brought the coffee anything like Moreni's size?" Sam asked.

"I never saw Moreni. The same guy went in and came out. I *know* that because I stopped him every time."

"What the Sam hell is going on!?" Dan demanded, and went to the desk. He returned a few minutes later with the manager and his passkey.

Moreni was across the bed with his wrists slashed and a bloody straight razor was on the floor beside him. The manager screamed like those women on TV who find bodies, so Dan took him out while Sam and I looked over the room carefully, then got a fairly good description of the one who brought coffee.

"We'd better get to Reynolds. Fast."

"I suppose he isn't in this part of it, is he? We'll get over there as soon as the lab boys arrive. Dan will handle this thing here. We're not going to find anything, unless it's some phony suicide note. I suppose, if Earl checks, he'll find something like a conk on the head."

"We're supposed to think it was a suicide and not look any further. Moreni's supposed to know we have him for killing Pratz and killed himself. Now the Farris bunch won't have to do it to be sure he doesn't make any deals."

"I hate to think Reynolds isn't in this!"

"He's in it, but we can't prove it. All we have is the bribe. That's not even part of this case."

"I don't suppose it really is, is it?"

"Zimmer had something in that video that ended up tying all these people together, but there are two different groups with two different dangers hanging over them. One group has all but eliminated itself. The other wants to finish the job.

"WHO, DAMN IT?! We don't have a clue!"

"We have a clue, but we can't see it. It's in that video, somewhere.

"Here's the lab van. Let's go see Reynolds."

"Mr. Reynolds, I don't think you understand what's going

on here. It's not about some stupid bribe," Sam said.

"I don't have any least idea what you're talking about," Reynolds sneered. "I simply met with some people at a construction site and gave them some architectural plans. This is ridiculous!"

"Come on, Sam," I said. We'd been trying to get through to Reynolds for over half an hour and he was stubbornly hanging on to his story. He wouldn't budge from the bribery part of it.

"I can't offer you police protection if you refuse your own information," Sam warned. "You're the only player left to kill, because you're the only other one we have in this mess. With you dead and out of the way, the killer's safe. Good day, Mr. Reynolds. I hope you live to see another one."

We went out and to Sam's car where he sat swearing for a long minute. He finally said, "I have to try to protect that sleazy scuzzbag, no matter how hard he tries to fight me."

"I don't think for one minute he's in any danger. He overdid it in there."

"You mean he's really the one behind it, after all?"

"No, but he *is* involved and he *does* know all about it."

He gave me a funny look and started the car.

We drove on back to the offices, where I got a copy of the videotape, then headed to my place to study it.

OK. Sean and Lorna found a body and reported it to the Marine Patrol.

Lorna called me, I came up and was out there before they'd finished with the scene.

The Marine Patrolman said it was a drug deal gone wrong and Sam said about the same thing, at first, but we determined that Zimmer had never had anything to do with drugs or drug dealers in any way, even peripherally, so we eliminated that, right away.

Zimmer was hit in an almost professional manner.

We searched Zimmer's place and found the videotape, which led us straight to the bribery part.

Reynolds, Moreni, Pratz and DuMont. Reynolds and DuMont were the two surviving.

Dan had seen Pratz around the construction sites before when he was investigating complaints about drug deals.

Wait a minute. Chronology.

The day before, as well as the morning of the murder, Dan had gone over to the subdivision where Zimmer worked, answering an anonymous tip about drugs. He found nothing.

Zimmer then took the videos near the house with the big black 34 on the side, apparently because he was the one who had made the tips about drug deals and was determined to get the proof for himself. The bribery thing suddenly started happening and he switched over to that and was seen, so Pratz and Moreni killed him.

We found the tape and tagged them with the bribery thing and soon would tag Pratz and Moreni with the murder.

We set up the scam to tag them with the bribe-taking.

DuMont ratted out Pratz and his alibi.

Why?

Someone thought there was something on that videotape. It was something Pratz and Moreni could call to our attention. They got rid of Pratz and Moreni, first trying to make the killing of Pratz look like a professional hit, yet done just poorly enough that we'd immediately jump on

Moreni.

Why?

Then a professional hit man did come to take care of Moreni. He was probably the same one who took care of Pratz.

Why?

Something else wasn't fitting very well now: Why did that Marine Patrolman say he'd seen Zimmer out in the gulf with drug runners? We knew very well Zimmer didn't have anything to do with those kinds of people.

I suddenly had a lot of questions about that patrolman.

I put the tape in the VCR and put it on the big screen in the Florida room to run it from the start. It was the same thing I'd seen several times already, so I tried to focus on details we hadn't paid attention to before. I was sure Sam was trying to identify all the people who came and went, but they seemed to be ordinary average working people – except for one big Lincoln Town Car that stopped. The chauffeur went into the house while the car sat at the curb with the motor running. There was someone inside, but the windows were blackened and I couldn't see anything but dark shadows.

I ran the tape through carefully, but the license plate never showed, though a plate in the front showed once that said "Paradise Shores" in white over green. It was a lengthened limousine that wouldn't be hard to find, if necessary.

I ran the tape on.

Nothing of any significance until the cut away from the house preparatory to focusing on the bribe scene. Various cars and trucks, one black Blazer with official light rails on top came by twice before the transaction, traveling slowly, and once during the bribe it crossed in the background.

That Lincoln was sitting across the empty lot beside the house diagonally south of the scene. A rear window was partly open, a face showed in it for a moment, then the scene zoomed to Reynolds and party and it was out of focus.

I stopped it at the face and expanded as much as I could. All that could be seen was a head with somewhat long, very black hair. It was too blurred to see anything else.

I wanted to know who owned that car, all of a sudden. Someone was watching the same group who had earlier appeared at the 34 house where the drug deals were going down. That car spelled money, so it was probably some local rich big shot. It could be someone who would have a bunch of people killed to avoid being identified as having been at that place at that time.

Horse, if you'll excuse the expression, manure! Whoever was in that car could very well have seen something, so I did want to talk to him. I was already sure this was one of those cases that were two separate things that touched at the wrong point at the wrong time. It often turned out that one case led to another.

Pratz and Moreni killed Zimmer for taping a bribe that could jeopardize a crime syndicate and a big developer. The developer was in it up to his ears, but we'd never be able to prove it.

That was the first case. It was solved and finished, but for the mopping.

Pratz and Moreni were killed to protect someone else. I didn't think it was Reynolds. I was now working on a separate case. My only clue to what it was had to do with what was on that tape – or what someone *feared* might be on the tape. I'd make a hell of a lot faster progress if I worked on it on that basis.

I looked up Paradise Shores on a city map. It was an old-money part of Southwest Naples – with a capital money. I hoped there weren't a lot of extended silver Lincolns with those plates on the front driving around out there. It wouldn't at all surprise me, the way things were going.

Chapter five

I drove around awhile, but most places in Paradise Shores were walled and back from the road. I'd passed a security gate when I first went in, showed the guards my Florida Grand Jury Marshal's papers, and they let me in without comment. I don't think they had instructions to notify anyone specific if the law came. They seemed disinterested in me and didn't appear to feel anyone in Snob Acres ever did anything they could be investigated for.

This was getting nowhere, so I went back to the gate and asked the guards about the Lincoln on the video.

"If you mean the extended black limousine, that would be Ed Camino over on Red Hibiscus Drive," one of them said. "Go along Sand Dollar Lane until you come to Sailfin Boulevard, turn right and it's the second right. Ed has the place on the end on the canal. Dark blue roof."

I thanked him and headed back.

The place had those dark blue fiberglass tiles on the roof and was a little larger than the new shopping center at 41 and Bonita Beach Road. Classy, but vulgar.

I pushed the button by the call box at the gate, informed the voice I was CD Grimes and I was looking for an Ed Camino. The gate opened and I drove up to the house.

A sort of hood/butler came out to escort me into the big house and on up to meet Ed Camino, who was a slightly fat Latin/Indian with somewhat long very dark black hair and a perpetually happy sort of face. He was wearing all kinds of rings and gold chains. He had attractive women running around the place, all of them with a lot of makeup on while most of whom didn't need it.

"Grimes? You the dick in the papers all the time?"

"A lot more than I want to be."

"Any special reason you came calling?"

"I'm investigating a murder of a construction worker over at that development by the Imperial River in Bonita. You were at the place when he filmed some local officials and P. P. Reynolds exchanging some bribe money. I was wondering if maybe you saw anything that could tie this stupid thing up. Seems all the witnesses so far have turned up dead."

"So you come calling on me?" he said with a happy grin. "Maybe I can be the next dead witness?"

"That would solve some peoples' problems, I suppose." I answered, matching the grin.

"Yeah! It wouldn't break too many hearts. Who fingered me as being there?"

"You were in the background of the tape watching the bribe from the back seat of your car, leaning out of the window."

"How about that? Care for a drink?"

"Not while I'm working. You in on the bribery thing, somehow?"

"Nah. It didn't have anything to do with any bribe, but none of that bunch could say anything about that. Bribes are way short of what was going down there. Reynolds doesn't have anything to do with any stupid bribes out in the open like that. He hires people to do that stuff for him. I'd tell you not to get involved with it, because the people concerned will handle it themselves in their own way, but you ain't gonna listen to me."

"It have to do with the coke?"

"Mostly. Stay out of it."

"I'll have to finish it. I don't think you had them trashed, but I think you know who did. My problem is that Zimmer was basically innocent and he ended up dead. Give me a name I can work on and I'll be out of your hair faster."

"None of it bothers me. I don't care if you're in it or not. I had my gripes and they're settled. Reynold's supposed to perform a certain service and he's supposed to see there are no complications. He got tied up with some bad people in what we'll call a competing branch of the business. They tried to squeeze him, and that would have been a minor inconvenience to me. It's been handled now, and none of my part had to do with anything in this state – in this particular deal. I own the right people in the right places and don't let any of it bother me. I deal the top and they deal with each other and don't even know it. I don't get involved with this kind of murder. It's far worse than stupid. I would never have anything to do with anything like that. It don't pay. All it could ever do is get your ass in a crack."

We chatted a few more minutes, then I left.

I could see who and what Ed was, a big supplier from somewhere – Peru. There was enough evidence of that around his house. He had supplied coke to the wholesalers and his local distributors were being moved in on by the Farris Franchise. He took care of that in his own way and considered the case closed.

I could see he'd been at the construction site to be sure that Reynolds cut Farris and friends out. That's what the exchange was about. It wasn't any bribe. It was why no one could talk about anything. That meant Pratz and DuMont were in on that bit, too. All of a sudden there was one hell of a piece missing. Camino brought the stuff in and Reynolds and company weren't distributing it properly?

That didn't make sense. Camino wouldn't care, one way or the other. If the Farris Franchise was buying or someone else, he got his. Farris was obviously getting Camino's product without having to pay Camino for it, which meant that.... The piece fell right into place. I knew what we'd missed all along and why things were said and done as they were. I stopped a few feet before I got to the gate and backed up to the house. Ed came outside with his big grin and asked what I'd forgotten.

"Was there interference before the stuff ever reached the shore?"

He laughed and slapped his knee. "I wondered if you'd catch it! Let's say someone working for someone else knew too much and was in a good position to insert himself into the main operation, which led me to the realization someone else *was* in it. I don't believe in too many coincidences. If there're too many of 'em, there ain't no coincidences. It was an offshore insertion."

I saluted, he grinned and waved, and I drove on out. All the inconsistencies were now neatly in line and fully explained.

I stopped at Lorna and Sean's to ask about Johnny's reputation among the local fishermen.

"Well, he's all right, I guess," Sean said. "He spends most of his time in the gulf, so he doesn't much bother us fishermen. Some of the Marine Patrol are asses, some are great people, and most are neutral. That's true of most things. Any organization that will give men guns and tell them they're little tin gods has one or two who're jerks."

"Now, Sean," Lorna chided. "They have their jobs to do."

"I know how you feel. I'm getting tired of not having anywhere I can go or anything I can do where some goon with a gun doesn't come to ask what I'm doing, but that's part of modern politics. It gets worse every year."

We didn't get into my opinions of how much closer to a police state we're becoming while Europe and even China and Russia are becoming more democratic.

I went to the Jeep and home, fixed a snack, checked the orchid houses, and sat in the den to consider. I wanted to know a hell of a lot more about our Marine Patrol officer who was so sure it would be a waste of the taxpayers' money to investigate Zimmer's murder. I wanted to know why he was so sure he saw Zimmer with drug smugglers on several occasions when Zimmer hadn't ever been anywhere near that kind of thing. I wanted to know why so many people seemed to know what the police were doing and where they got their information. It all added up one way. Zimmer was killed because of those tapes, not because of any bribery scheme. The same ones were involved. Pratz and Moreni had killed Zimmer, but then someone else had killed Moreni and Pratz.

Ed Camino was a drug supplier from Peru. He made no attempt whatever to hide that fact. There was some kind of deal where his crap was being intercepted before it got to Florida and he as much as told me Johnny was behind it.

Contact man – or boss?

Zimmer's connection was at the house with the 34 on the side. I thought of that black Blazer with the blue lights on top going by twice before and once while the deal was going down out there. That was a Marine Patrol wagon. I was sure we could get that from the tape. I called Lorna and asked what Johnny's full name was.

"Either Wilson or Williams," she said, then asked Sean, who said it was Wilson. I thanked her and hung up.

Next was a call to Sam to ask him to check on Wilson as quietly as possible. The next running of the tape indicated what I'd already decided, so I went out in the boat for a little while. I came back in and called Lydia for a bit of an appointment. She said she'd like to get away for awhile, so came over to the house for the meeting. She was greatly impressed with the place, particularly with the painting of Mike Nelson over the big TV screen in the living room.

I told her what I thought, she considered a bit, then called Lou Prinz. They argued some, then she said Lou was going to let out a wee hint to a specific person about a certain important developer who possibly might have made a deal with the police for relocation under the witness protection plan – just a rumor, you know.

Lou was going to meet us in an hour and a half at Charlene's Restaurant, over by the dog track. Lydia didn't know what Lou was planning to do, but he'd investigated a lot about Reynolds. He'd said it would bring the pot to a boil if the person he thought was telling other people about news stories before they reached print really was.

We headed for Charlene's. We got a table 'way in the back room and waited. Lou showed up twenty minutes later and said to tell Sam to watch Reynolds very carefully. If he'd let the right rumor out to the right person, two things were going to happen:

Reynolds would be marked for murder.

A certain copy girl would find it impossible to ever again find a job with any newspaper in the US or abroad.

"I let it slip to a press liaison officer where that certain copy girl could hear that Reynolds is tied up tight and will be spilling his guts to try to save his own crooked ass," Lou reported. "If what you figure is right, they'll have to get Reynolds before he talks. It has to be done today. I hinted Reynolds was going to start his talking tonight."

Lydia said she thought that girl was the one who was spreading tales, so she'd turn the heat up a degree or two. She explained, "I'll call Betty and tell her to take a story about something that's going to happen tonight and can't be released until it's done. Add it to what you said, maybe somebody will panic.

"I'll say CD says DuMont's been playing games with them and they tripped him up. He stands to collect a hell of a lot from Reynolds for the rest of his life, but the evidence he hid has been found and the police are sorting it out now. Reynolds is caught and will make a deal to save his own worthless crooked hide because he didn't kill anyone – but he damned well knows who did! His only chance to stay out of the pen for ten to fifteen is to spill."

"DuMont? I thought you had him and he'd be going up for sure," Lou said.

"I said from the first he'd make a deal, and he did. That thing about an alibi for Pratz was a clever way to admit involvement in something that's not of any major importance. He planned to appear willing to spill his guts about that kind of thing, make a deal, get probation or something, we'd mark the case solved, and he'd be set up to blackmail the rest of them for life."

"They'd kill him in a minute!" Lydia protested.

"Not if he's got solid evidence somewhere they can't get at it," Lou said, thinking. "If.. That's why he's still alive now! He *has* the evidence! HE'S the one...!

"You call Betty. Tie Reynolds to DuMont for her. Tight! That's what the others will believe. He's already let them know he has the evidence, or he'd already be dead.

"Great lord! If we can find that evidence we can get every stinking last one of them!"

We discussed that while Lydia called in. She came back, and asked, "Does this mean DuMont's really in this as deep as the others?"

"I think DuMont and Reynolds are in it as the top dogs, but in the second thing, not in the killing of Zimmer. I don't think the others know that. If they do, they won't fall for this scam. I think friend DuMont found something really big when he was inspecting something for Reynolds and cut himself in at the top."

"Ah-ha! Now it makes sense!" Lydia cried. "Reynolds and Moreni were on that tape handing the case to DuMont! Pratz looked inside and drooled, but the case was handed to DuMont, not *him*! Does that mean Tate DuMont was already in cahoots with Reynolds?"

"All we have is a lot of speculation. I think Camino put pressure on Reynolds to get Farris out of the deal and that bit was for the edification of Moreni. I think Moreni was told it was out of their hands, now. Pratz was going to be running things, Pratz had the goods on them all and it was in a safe place – and there wasn't going to be anything left for Farris, so Moreni was to go back up north and say it wasn't worth the effort to try to fight.

"Zimmer was caught taking the video. Moreni wasn't in a position where the Farris Franchise could be tied into it. He was to become the sacrificial goat to head Camino off at the pass. Moreni, being a hood of that particular type, conveniently pressured Pratz into helping him take care of

Zimmer.

"That started the second phase of it. It came about because, suddenly, one group didn't know what the other was doing, or why. Threats or something earlier made the second group afraid the first group knew a lot of things they did *not* know.

"That cost Pratz his life. Things fell apart faster and faster until it came to now. Everyone feels reasonably safe, so long as DuMont keeps his mouth shut. If DuMont blabs, only Reynolds can tie Johnny into it. They'll *have* to sacrifice Johnny, who has been intercepting the drugs in the gulf and bringing them in aboard his Marine Patrol boat to the Reynolds subdivision, where they were being distributed through house thirty four. The drugs were really the property of Ed Camino. He walked in on them a few minutes before the video was made and laid down the law, hard, leaving DuMont and Reynolds in one hell of a mess.

"That was the one coincidence in the whole fiasco. It's what caused the rest to happen. It caused all the later confusion. They all jumped to wrong conclusions or it would have stopped with Zimmer. DuMont and Reynolds thought, if they could get rid of Farris, they could deal with Camino and keep going, just as they were. It would be him instead of another big syndicate head to cut into their profits, but Camino would bring in his own private army to wipe them out if they didn't agree to that.

"You see, Camino traced the one who was taking the drugs out in the gulf and followed Johnny to that house. Ed Zimmer had the horrible misfortune to choose the day Reynolds and DuMont pulled their own scam to dump Farris to take his videos, then Ed Camino came in, doubled the pressure, and added confusion. There wasn't anywhere to turn. Zimmer had to be gotten rid of and it started getting worse and worse.

"Now the killer can feel safe unless Reynolds talks. That won't happen. The only real pressure we can put on him is through DuMont, and DuMont won't break.

"In the past hour or so our killer learns DuMont *is* going to talk and Reynolds has already promised a deal!"

"Ed Camino is in this? Is he group one or two or both?" Lou asked.

"That's what no one knows."

"I get it!" Lydia cried.

"He's the supplier who was getting ripped off for the drugs, in the first place,. That's where Johnny Wilson came in. He would take a percent of the stuff and let the rest of it go on up past Tampa. They give him trouble and they get the rest of it seized and end up in the calaboose, on top of it. It's part of doing that kind of business here. Farris trying to cut in meant Johnny had to double what he got to stay where he was and Camino put and end to it. It was getting beyond normal business expenses.

"Johnny won't have much of a past, I think. He knew too much about how to throw suspicion on Moreni and he knew how to make Pratz look like a deliberate hit that was meant to look like a hit.

"I wonder where he's from."

"Chicago. He killed Moreni?" Lydia asked.

"Maybe we'll find out. I think Farris was getting damned worried Moreni was a tie that would sink him and had that done. If so, we'll never get his killer, simply because he *was* a professional hit and *will* be back in some other state by now. I'm not going to worry over that one."

"That's part of getting involved with those people," Lou said. "It had to be like that, because Johnny would know killing Moreni wouldn't do him any good. It's DuMont who was the big threat, and he can't get to him. The only way to neutralize DuMont is to get Reynolds."

"How do you figure?" Lydia asked.

"Isn't it obvious? DuMont can only tie Pratz and Moreni to *Camino*. Only Reynolds can tie it all to dear little Johnny. Johnny has to figure, if DuMont really does start talking, he'll implicate Camino. He knows full well Camino isn't going to implicate anybody."

"Yes. Which proves Moreni was hit on orders from Farris," Lou agreed. "No one else could give a damn about him. He was out and headed back home."

"Camino said that it was already handled. I think he might have deliberately caused the extra confusion so the competition would get rid of each other. How long before anything happens with this thing? We've been here for more than two hours!"

"All of it hangs on Johnny hearing about our little tips. He has to get Reynolds, because Reynolds is the only person in the world who can bring it all right back to him," Lydia answered. "I may be slow, but I *do* get there.

"Why are we here, Lou?"

"Because Reynolds is at the track," Lou said, simply.

"I see," Lydia said. "I don't think Wilson will know he's out here. I didn't say anything to leak back about that. Did you?"

"No, but Reynolds never misses Wednesday Matinee at the track," Lou replied. "Everyone knows that. Wilson will know it.

"I wonder how much longer it'll be before we know if the

plan worked. The races will be over in about half an hour."

Sam and Dan came in about ten minutes later to say they caught Johnny Wilson putting two sticks of dynamite under the seat of Reynolds' car, wired to the ignition. He'd had Dan following him ever since my call to have him checked on, so knew where to find him when Lou called them to say they should watch Reynolds every second.

"It was pretty much the way you figured," Dan said, handing me a cup of coffee. Lydia and Lou had left the restaurant to take in their scoops and we were back at the sheriff's station. "Miko Sarasvati was staying at the motel where Moreni was the night before he was killed. We can put him right there at the motel."

"Who's Miko Whatever?"

"We've been watching for anybody from Detroit who has any ties with the Farris Franchise," Sam said. "He's a muscle they've used before a few times. We didn't spot him when he came in, but we found where he stayed right there at the motel. The desk clerk identified him from the mug shots and we traced. He's already gone and we can't do anything about him, now. I don't think we can get any proof, but that's how it goes. *We* know."

"If Zimmer hadn't taken that video there would still be a pretty big drug operation going on up north of here," Sam said. "We'll be able to stop that one route, but we aren't going to be able to touch Camino.

"I guess he wasn't involved – in this part, anyhow. He'll have to move the operation elsewhere, I suppose. It's an expected part of the business."

"I'll try to do a little something about that. You've got this one sewed up tight?"

"Reynolds tagged Johnny for us because he was so mad – and really scared – about Johnny trying to blow his butt through his Landau roof," Dan agreed. "He heard a tip that DuMont was about to spill through some girl named Betty at the paper and got there first by putting DuMont in the middle. DuMont was so pissed-off he gave us the key to a safe deposit box that has enough crap in it to hang everyone concerned, implicate Farris, and maybe even get us some small things on Ed Camino. He was thorough. In return, he receives certain little immunities and the re-location by the witness protection thing. It was all he had left. He finally got the deal and will get away with it, pretty well, but he was more a bookkeeper and behind-the-scenes type, anyhow."

"I'm going to call on Ed Camino. You said you can't really stop him, but maybe I can. He really doesn't care, anymore. He has more money than he could hope to spend in his lifetime. He won't be giving up anything. He can claim it's gotten too hot to operate anymore, so his buyers can look elsewhere for a supplier. That's also a standard part of the business."

"We don't have much we can use on him. It's better than nothing," Sam agreed. "I wish we could put an end to his type."

"He's really a likeable sort. He sees himself as someone who gave employment to several hundred people back home who were being pushed around by their own government and ignored by ours. They'll have made enough now that they can get out of it and find a little farm or something, somewhere. He did a lot for those people and a hell of a lot more for Ed Camino."

We filled out all the papers and chatted awhile, then I

drove to Paradise Shores and announced myself at the gate. It swung open and I drove in to find Ed standing by the door.

"Still working?"

"Cuervo Gold and grapefruit juice in a tall glass with lots of ice."

"I got word you tagged that Reynolds bastard good. Thanks. Wilson was getting greedy beyond what was proper. He's a very nasty sort. Was the little tin bureaucrat really the brains?"

"A hell of a lot more than they're letting on," I answered, as we went inside, where a very nicelooking tall blonde handed me my drink.

"What does that mean?"

"You did me a favor. You told me a thing or two when you didn't have to tell me anything. When I owe a favor, I try to repay it.

"DuMont was collecting a lot of information all along about a hell of a lot of people. He collected solid proof, along with his information, so he would have a lever to put pressure on people later when he had his little business going. He could stay alive only if he had that proof where they couldn't get it.

"He has a lot of stuff the DEA's going to get greatly excited about. Various people who were, shall we say, sponsoring a small business venture, have some very solid things against them in that material. The information is now in the hands of the police and the FBI and DEA, except for a couple of things that fell off the desk or something when we were sorting it out for the various agencies. People who've done me some favors are implicated in ways they can't even guess in some very embarrassing situations. Those things can't be defended against – if the persons they're against are in this country or any other country with an extradition agreement with this country.

"When those items are found, in three days, they'll have to be turned over to the agencies they're marked for.

"This is very good tequila! It's not Cuervo, is it?"

"It's some stuff I have made special," Ed replied with a big grin. "I've been thinking about moving to my place on a little island I own and investing in the small distillery that makes the tequila for me.

"I hope you and your friends are safe before any wrong conclusions are drawn because of what DuMont may have left. It could lead to a very bloody conflict if one certain family in Detroit is in it – in fact, it will, regardless.

"I've only met you twice, but you seem the kind of person I could like. Maybe I'll send you my address after I've moved and settled in and you can come for a visit! I know you like orchids and water. The island has plenty of both!"

"I just might take you up on that!"

Don't Push

C. D. Moulton's works are available on most major outlets as printed or e-books. CD writes the CD Grimes, PI, mysteries, the Det. Lt. Nick Storie mysteries, the Clint Faraday mysteries, the Flight of the Maita science fiction series, books on orchid culture and many others of many types. Mystery, adventure, intrigue, science fiction, humor, fantasy, paranormal, mild erotica, and factual.